Dedicated to all Rochesterians

Past

Present

Future

A Gift for:

Presented By:

*Reading fiction stimulates our*

*imaginations and enriches our lives*

Also by J. A. Goodman

Emma Mason Mystery Series

*Tangled Justice* 2016

*Domestic Justice* 2017

*Legal Justice* 2018

FREE TO VIEW Short Stories @

www.SeniorsInk.com

Short stories ~ FICTION

*The Little Woman*

*The Irish Dreamer*

*The Journey Continues*

*When the Atheist Challenged God*

*Hey You Never Know*

Short stories ~ MEMOIRS

*A Position of Trust*

*The Dirty Mirror*

1

# TANGLED

# JUSTICE

J. A. GOODMAN

2

Text set in: Droid Serif
Cover by:  Argus Gray

Written in and about Rochester, New York
Printed in the United States of America
Createspace.com

ISBN-13: 978-1537558844
ISBN-10: 1537558846

To my daughter Barbara
whos knowledge and
encouragement
made this book possible.

# ADVANCE PRAISE

5

*"Very easy read, kept me on the edge of my seat until the last word. Character development is fabulous. Loved the Rochester location. I hope there's a sequel soon."*

~ J. W. Lindsay, Retired: Air Traffic Control Specialist


*"Suspenseful easy read detective novel, complete with many twists and turns. As I followed detective Emma Mason in her pursuit of an avenging killer, I couldn't put the book down. I'm looking forward to the next in what I hope will be a Series of Emma Mason detective adventures."*

~ Gail Lysenko, Retired Teacher


*"This book is a tense, satisfying story about use of forensic science, solving murders and romance."*

~ Larry and Suzanne Denison Kretovic, Former classmates, Charlotte High School, Class of 1960

# ACKNOWLEDGEMENTS AND THANKS

Many thanks to all the people who offered guidance, structure and most of all encouragement. Especially to my daughter Barbara, who read every line, every word and offered her invaluable input and support.

Professor Perri whose encouragement and kind words inspired me. Thanks to my friends who read the first or second drafts and gave me their valuable suggestions and opinions. They include Gail and Nick Lysenko, Sue and Larry Kretovic, Maureen Kelly, Carol Benedict and my cousin John Lindsay. I am grateful to my course leaders at Osher Lifelong Learning Institute; Pat Edelman from Express Yourself in Writing, Carol Samuel from the Memoirs Class and Donna M. Marbach from Writers' Critique. Special thanks to all my classmates at Osher, who listened to my stories and supplied different viewpoints. I would like to thank Argus Gray for putting together this colorful book cover and Mary Dougherty, for her advice in the field of Self-Publishing.

# INTRODUCTION

Accompany Detective Emma Mason and her partner, Mitch
Delaney, as they undertake to protect the city of Rochester, New
York from a psychopathic killer as he falls deep into the abyss of
his mental disorder.

Explore the world of police procedures, as they interact with the
crime unit, the coroner's office, ballistics and the patrol officers
who serve and protect. Read about real techniques, as well as
conceptual ones, I developed because they could certainly enhance
the repertoire of law enforcement should they be available in the
future. Woven into the story is the tale of a wealthy and mysterious
suitor named Peter, who appears to have fallen head over heels for
Emma. Travel with Emma as their two worlds collide in
unexpected ways. Emma's emotional struggle when she uncovers
information that points to him as a dangerous, international
criminal.This story is rich with investigative science and clips
along the streets of Rochester at an invigorating pace, highlighting
events that made the city famous. Readers looking for a smart,
entertaining mystery will not be disappointed.

# List of Characters

Alexander Chesterton Wright III ... Educated, Troubled

Emma Lynne Mason ............ RPD Homicide Unit

Mitch Delaney ............ Detective, former marine

Amanda ................. Dates Mitch sometimes


Jack Davis ................... Head of Crime Unit

Anne ........................... Jack's wife

Brett ........................... Member Crime Unit

Barbara ....................... Brett's wife


Luther John Maxwell ............... Criminal

Rick & Debby Jones ............ Maxwell's neighbors

Rose Marie Pacelli ............ Maxwell's neighbor


Doc Kyle MacGee ..................Medical Examiner

Carole ................................. Doc's wife

Jenny .. ...............................Doc's Daughter

Jean Doyle ......................... Emma's neighbor, friend

Peter Hartman .................... Businessman
Gordon Kleinman .............. Cook, bodyguard
Vera ................................. Gordon's wife
Paul Spears .................... Friend from Florida

Colleen Marks .......................
George Tyler ........................ Victims of Maxwell
Red Lemcke ..........................
Mr. Ronald Reed .................. Luther's Alibi
Mrs. Maxwell .......................Luther's Mother

Joe (Skiing) ..............
Sal (Scuba Diving) ..... Past Boyfriends of
John (Golfing) ........... Jean & Emma
Jerry (Dancing) ..........

Tyrone Williams .................. Teenagers found
Wayne Holden .................... Gun

Ted Bruggeman............... Entomologist

Detective O'Reilly ................ Retired

Officer Brigham .................. Desk Sergeant

Officer Geraci ................ Member of Emma's unit

Officer Carris ..................... Patrol officer

Sergeant Ziemba ............... Dispatch

Jamie and Christie ......... SPOT HOTS, Food Truck


Edward O. Jackson ......... Famous Tennis Player

Jimmie .......................... Bartender, Main Place


Ryan Kelly ....................... Peters Partner

Susan LaMonte ...............Peter's past girlfriend


Jethro Mercier ............ Killed Alexander's parents

Ginny Peckallo ............... Jethro's lady friend

Tony Stark ....................... Alexander's Alias

Accidental Al .................. Professional Killer

Don Newcomb ................. Special Agent, FBI

# CHAPTER 1

Alexander paused to glance behind him before he continued following the shadowy figure into the alley. Darkness descended like a curtain of black that enveloped him with every step. The stench of rotting garbage invaded his nostrils. He held his breath in a futile attempt to calm his emotions. He reconsidered the risk he was taking in this God-forsaken alley. Through no fault of his own, his survival, his very existence had descended to bring him here. His options were limited, but could he execute his plan? He signed, it was too late to go back. He had to continue or his world would be destroyed. He hurried his steps to catch up to Max, who had disappeared into the darkness.

Alexander had met Max less than a week ago when the man had literally walked out of the county courthouse and into Alexander's parked car. Max appeared to have been in a hurry to leave the building and was not paying attention to where he was going when he struck the car, bouncing off the fender and landing on the sidewalk. Max was limping when he stood up and tried to walk away. Alexander had felt obligated to offer him a ride. However, he was appalled when Max took him up on his proposition.

Max had become so excited, almost childlike, when he opened the door and eased his disheveled body into the comfortable leather seat. As they drove, Max ran his hands over the upholstery, opened and closed the lighted vanity mirror, inspected the gadgetry on the dash. He gushed as he complimented Alexander's taste in vehicles, barely able to contain his excitement at being driven around in a luxury car. He scarcely took a breath as he shared the myriad and sordid details of his pathetic life. Alexander wrote Max off as a low-brow thug in a bad suit disgorging non sequiturs in a feeble attempt to be interesting. The thing that piqued Alexander's interest was when

Max bragged about how successful he was at evading justice, not just once, but numerous times, including that very day.

When Alexander approached the address Max had indicated, he was surprised to see Max pull out an enormous wad of bills from the pocket of his coat. He offered to pay Alexander for the ride, making a show of how well he did for himself with his petty crimes. Alexander declined, but couldn't deny that the wad of cash had been most attractive. Max couldn't have known how tempted Alexander was to pluck that bundle of cash out of his hands and drive away. Instead, Alexander refused the offer but suggested they meet the next day for coffee.

Now here they were, four days later, in this dark, foul smelling alley. Alexander paused for a second to allow his eyes time to adjust to the dark. He felt the blood racing through his veins. Experiencing danger was a completely new sensation and Alexander was enjoying the unexpected thrill this rush of adrenalin was producing. It made him feel so alive, something other than that dull, hollow feeling he had learned to endure since his parents had been murdered.

The alley they had slipped into was a dead end and Max was proudly showing Alexander the way. "Well, watdaya think?" Max whispered, using his hands in a sweeping gesture, to encompass the area. "Is dis the perfect place for a muggin' or what! Like, I can't believe I never found dis spot before... the times I musta walked right by. Man, look, no glass... jest brick... great, huh? Tonight's gonna be my... ah... I mean our night. What luck to find dis place, you'll see... once our eyes gets used ta the dark I mean. Well... watdaya think, pal?"

Alexander sometimes had difficulty understanding Max's communication style. He knew they were speaking the same language, however, Alexander's vernacular was the result of the best private schools money could buy, while it was obvious that Max's formal education had ended early, and his unique dialect had been picked up on the street.

"I'm constantly impressed with your enterprising nature, Max, nevertheless I'm unaccustomed to these dismal surroundings. I especially dislike the horrific smell coming from... God knows what." He paused, trying not to think about the cause of the repulsive stench that filled the air. "I anticipate I may have difficulty adapting to your methods in order to survive. Psychologically, um... what I mean is, in your mind Max, how do you suppress your morality after inflicting this random violence unto your unfortunate victims? What I am trying to say is, I'm wondering... how do you reconcile your conscience?"

Max looked puzzled as he removed his hat to wipe his brow, then replaced it before answering. "My conscience? I'm not sure I got one of those." he said slowly. "My Mother was always yelling at me. I think she was trying ta tell me right from wrong, but she gave up when I stole the welfare lady's wallet the day she come ta see if we was poor 'nuff fer that there free money they're always tryin' ta give away. I jest took mine without all the paperwork they want ya ta fill out. Sides, who says I'm not a good guy? Even God says he helps them that helps themselves, don't he? Wasn't my fault my old man run off with that there whore, but that didn't stop Ma from blamin' us kids. I took off soon is I found this here gun hidden up on the roof. This gun gives me all the power I'll ever need." He patted his bulging pocket, then added, "I help Ma out with money now and then, ya know, so I'm what ya'd call a good son."

Alexander thought he should feel sympathetic, perhaps even compassion but he felt only apathy. "Indeed Max. I believe I shall investigate the interior of this alley to make sure we are indeed, alone."

"The interior? Oh, ya mean the back? Ya, sure, but be careful."

Alexander left Max and moved into the darkest part of the alley, taking slow, deep breaths in an attempt to calm his growing nervousness. He looked for any sign of life that might be hiding in the dark recesses of this fetid place. As he stepped further into the alley, he took great care not to step into anything that could leave an imprint of his footwear. It wasn't just because he didn't want to leave any evidence behind, but perhaps, just as important, they were Italian leather! He could not imagine having to remove this dreadful muck from his expensive footwear. The days of having everything cleaned for him by willing servants were long gone. He'd have to do it himself and almost gagged at the thought. Next time, he would know better, he would acquire shoes that he could throw away when he was done.

His mind cruised back over the lessons he had learned in his Forensic Science Courses that described in great detail how police detectives and criminal investigation units combed over crime scenes with amazing thoroughness. How they used modern scientific methods of crime detection and forensic science to uncover the tiniest clues to trip up the uneducated criminals. He thought it was incredible that he was now applying that knowledge to avoid being caught by the very people he had once wanted to emulate. His carefree college days seemed a lifetime ago.

An explosion of garbage interrupted Alexander's thoughts. Before he could react, a large, rat ran between his legs and disappeared. A second followed the first, running over Alexander's shoe before disappearing into a pile of boxes stacked against the wall. Panic began to build inside his slender frame. He wasn't sure if it was the sudden appearance of the rats or his uncertainty over the path his life was taking. He fought to slow his breathing to a steady rhythm. He could still control that, it was the rest of his life that seemed to be spinning down this path that fate had decreed. His thoughts centered on his losses over the last two years. The senseless murder of his parents, brutally beaten to death in their own home. Following that, the loss of the family business. He was unable to stop the lawyers and business partners, that his father had trusted, from taking everything, leaving him overwhelmed and desperate for money. He knew in his heart, this was all their fault.

His panic ebbed as he reexamined his plan. He raised his face toward the sky and asked for guidance from the two men who had entrusted him to carry on their name. A feeling of determination and resolve seemed to enter his body, beginning at the top of his head and rolling like water, down to the bottom of his feet. He was after all, Alexander Chesterton Wright the Third, and proud of his name. Proud to share it with those two extraordinary men. Alexander turned and moved with new resolve and determination, away from the rats, back to the mouth of the alley where Max was waiting.

"I have concluded that other than a few rats, this alley is unoccupied. What's your typical strategy? What I mean is, what do we do next?" Alexander fumbled for uncomplicated words that he thought Max would understand.

"My typical strategy? I love the way ya talk, Alex." Max had been slouched against the wall but stood up straight, grinning with pride. "I get a kick outa havin someone like you ask me what ta do. Course, I am pretty good at this, been on my own sixteen years now, since I was 15 and I found this here gun. Hey, I'm jest thinkin', could you stop calling me Max and call me Luther? My name's Luther Maxwell. Max is a nickname. Like, don't ya think it sounds better? Luther and Alexander, I like it way better."

Alexander chuckled to himself at Max's suggestion but said nothing.

"Anyway, it's like this… first we wait 'til the street's not crowded. When we see somebody walking alone, we just jump out, quick cover their mouth, an' pull 'em in here. We might hafta knock 'em around a bit till they give up their valuables, but sometimes they jest start bawlin' and then it's a piece a cake... they toss everything at you and run away. Done it lotsa times… got lotsa money in my pocket to prove it too! We'll split everything we get tonight, say... fifty fifty? Okay partner? That's fair! All we gotta do is wait."

Alexander remembered waiting for the doctors in the hospital and those horrid pills. Now that they had released him, he didn't have enough money to fill the prescriptions. He'd convinced himself that he was better off without the pills. They clouded his mind and muddled his thoughts when he needed a clear head. He was confident that if he were still taking them, he would not have uncovered this pathway to redemption. He shifted his weight as he recalled with sadness all the events that had led to this alley and the destiny that he and Max now shared.

"Hey, Alex, a penny for your thoughts."

"Ah, you know Max, I'm sorry, em, Luther, I was just thinking, after tonight, there is no going back." Alexander gave himself a shake as if the physical movement would clear his thoughts. He shifted his weight before he continued. "Luther, you say you possess a weapon... er... I mean a piece. Have you ever... well... had to resort to violence when committing these felonies?"

"Ya mean plug the jerks? Sure, ya never know when some dumb shit is gonna... make things... well, harder for me than it should be. There was this college girl once, said she wouldn't give up her engagement ring, said she'd die first, so I had to shoot her. Boy oh boy, sometimes people are so dumb, even the educated ones." Max shook his head and smiled as he recalled the event.

"You shot a woman over a ring?" Alexander felt a mixture of repulsion and fascination.

"Was her choice! It was a big diamond," Max defended his decision.

Alexander had learned enough, he was ready. Standing alongside Max, Alexander thought about the gun in Max's pocket. He didn't like the idea of using a gun. His parents had never allowed him to have even a toy gun growing up. He wasn't sure how comfortable he would be actually using one, but he reasoned that he needed the money, and it's not like Max didn't understand the ultimate power of that gun.

Alexander glanced around the alley one more time and had to give Max credit, it was the perfect spot for a crime, any crime.

"Luther, could you stand closer and let me examine your gun for a minute?"

"Sure thing pal. Glad to see ya taking so much interest in the details. We're going ta make a great team, like Butch Cassidy and the Sundance Kid."

Max handed the gun over to Alexander with great care. "Easy now, it's loaded. I don't want ya shootin' yourself. This one's got a hair trigger, I filed it myself."

"Don't worry, I have no intention of harming myself." Alexander took the gun from Max with both hands. He positioned it between them, held his breath and pulled the trigger.

Alexander was impressed that it took only the slightest pressure to fire the gun. He felt a satisfying and peaceful calm engulf him even as he saw the surprised look in Max's eyes, seconds before the spark of life disappeared. He watched Max's lifeless body transform to the consistency of a rag doll, as it dropped to the asphalt, where it took up residence, crumpled into a twisted, shapeless heap against the wall.

Alexander removed his new leather gloves, revealing a second pair of latex gloves underneath. He worked the new leather gloves onto Max's motionless fingers then searched Max's body looking for money. He was pleased when he found the large roll of bills Max kept in his jacket pocket. He located his wallet and removed that money as well. Using care, he replaced the wallet. Alexander wanted the police to know whose body they'd found but there was no point in leaving any money behind. After all, Alexander needed it, with all the overdue bills, current expenses and of course a donation to the church. Mother would insist that he continue giving generous donations to the church.

His final task was to stage the gun in Max's gloved hand. Alexander took a step backwards to admire his work, then decided to topple a couple loose bags to conceal the top half of Max's body. He hoped the police would call it a suicide, although a few might hope some innocent victim had turned the tables on this remorseless murderer.

Alexander removed his latex gloves and slipped them into the pocket of his new plastic raincoat. He would destroy the coat and gloves tomorrow. The hint of a smile crept onto his lips as he felt the first drop of rain fall on his face. A powerful storm was moving in, just as the weatherman had predicted. The rain would wash the blood splatter off his coat in no time, everything was falling into place.

The rain intensified as Alexander strode out of the alley and down the now deserted streets. He walked several blocks before boarding a bus that would take him to his car. What a night, he thought. He had never felt so alive, even jubilant now that he had rid the world of that poor misguided creature. What a thrill it had been to watch life disappear as Max faded into oblivion. It actually felt invigorating, even rejuvenating. Yes, that's it, he felt like a new man. He knew he had found his destiny.

'Too bad I can't explain to my doctors how great I feel! How well I'm coping!' he thought. But that could never happen. He knew he couldn't tell them. They wouldn't understand. They would probably send him back to that awful place. They might think he was still crazy.

## CHAPTER 2

The call came in Monday morning at 6:45 am. Two teenage boys were in an alley sneaking a smoke when they discovered a body. Emma was thankful she hadn't eaten breakfast before arriving on scene. She surmised from the smell of decomposition that the body had been there for a few days. Hard to tell though, since the alley was full of garbage in various stages of decay, along with what appeared to be several well fed rats. The M.E. would be able to tell her more when he examined the body in the morgue. What was left of it, that is… after the rats.

Emma looked up and saw Mitch heading further into the alley searching for evidence. Mitch Delaney was her best detective, a 13-year veteran who often unearthed clues that others had missed. He possessed a mind that not only thought outside the box, but lived there. If there was anything worth discovering in the dark recesses of that alley, she was confident he would find it. Mitch was a little over 6 feet tall and 220 pounds of toned muscle. He still wore his dark hair in the style of the Marines with whom he had served with pride, after graduating high school. He moved with a confident stride borne of experience and self-discipline that many women found irresistible. His piercing light brown eyes matched his skin tone and his good looks always demanded a double take wherever he roamed. She assumed he had inherited those good looks from his French father while his skin tone was given to him by his mother who was born in Africa, the daughter of missionaries. Mitch had been born and raised in America, but was well versed in several languages thanks to his parents' extensive travels.

Emma studied the remains while the photographer continued to document the scene. She surmised, from the look of the body, the man had died right here, just before or during the heavy rainstorm on Thursday evening. The rain had poured down in torrents for more than five hours that night and she knew that would make evidence collection difficult, if not impossible. She turned on her recorder and started to document her observations. "Detective Emma Mason, RPD, date May 11, 2015, 7:18 am. Body of a white male, approximately 5'9", 190 pounds, appears to have been shot once through the heart. Powder burns on the clothing around the wound."

The photographer signaled that she was finished. Emma pulled on a pair of latex gloves, bent down to search his pockets, and found a wallet with ID. She read aloud, "Luther Maxwell, born September 21, 1984," then reached for his hand to verify. She removed his glove and placed his hand on the fingerprint screen, rolling each of his fingers. The screen flashed and the identification was verified using the mobile Integrated Automated Fingerprint Identification System or IAFIS for short. Further inquiry revealed that Luther Maxwell had a long history with the department starting out as a juvenile offender when he was just twelve years old.

Mitch was working his way back to Emma and the body. "It looks like the storm washed away any evidence. My father would have said, *'Il pleut comme vache qui pisse'* or loosely translated, it was raining like a pissing cow."

Emma shook her head, "your father had some interesting sayings Mitch, but I'm more interested in what you have to say about this body."

Mitch looked down at the body with a discerning eye. "Well, the rats were just beginning to nibble on his ears. Another day and his entire face could have been gone just like other parts of his body."

"Yeah, lucky for us he died at this end of the alley and those bags covered his face. Another bit of luck is that he was wearing those gloves or I wouldn't have had fingers to verify ID."

"Well, it might be nothing, but those look like expensive new gloves. Why would a guy with such shabby clothing be wearing brand new leather gloves? Especially this time of year. Where would he have bought them? The stores changed over to spring and summer wear months ago."

"That caught my eye too, but with shopping on the internet so prevalent, seasonal goods have gone the way of public phone booths."

"That's going back, wonder how Superman would change his clothes nowadays?"

"Simple Mitch, he would drive one of those windowless vans."

"That makes sense, then with his X-ray vision he could see if anyone was in the area before he jumped out and flew away."

"Mitch, focus. Murder investigation here." She noted the silly grin on his face. "Why aren't you bothered by the smell? My stomach's been doing summersaults."

Mitch reached into his pocket and pulled out a small jar of Vicks. "Here you go, just put a little under your nose, works every time."

"You always carry Vicks?" She opened the jar and spread a big glob of it under her nose before giving the jar back.

"Never can tell when you'll need it in our business."

"You didn't find the murder weapon?"

"No, just the one casing next to the body. Looks like a 38." Mitch knelt alongside the body looking it over once more. "Hey Em, did you notice the gunpowder on the glove you removed from his right hand? That's odd. It would indicate he either held the gun and shot it at some point before he died, or he shot himself and someone made off with the gun."

"Remind me to verify with Doc MacGee if Maxwell was right handed. We'll need to talk to those teenagers again. My preliminary search of the body turned up a wallet in his back pocket with ID, but no money, no phone, no car keys. I did find house keys. Hopefully they'll jibe with the address on his license. Looks like he's wearing an expensive watch. If it was robbery, why would the killer or killers leave the watch?"

"You're assuming he had money in his wallet, but maybe he was broke and met someone back here that was going to give him money. Or maybe his gloves concealed the watch, or his killer just missed it. Weird. Is the guy a bum or not? Expensive watch, expensive gloves, crappy clothes, cheap shoes"

"I know, maybe he just shot himself accidently when he was aiming at the rats. Anything's possible at this point."

"You mean like when people have their cameras turned backwards and end up taking a picture of their nose instead of what they wanted? Now that would be one for the books."

"It would indeed." She continued to examine the man's driver's license. "Okay, we're done here, let's turn this over to the Crime Unit while we check out this address... see what we can turn up that might help. On the way, check with motor vehicles to see if he owned a car to go with this license." Emma switched off her recorder and put it back in her pocket. She looked over at Jack and raised her voice to get his attention "Jack, we're clear, you and your crew can have the alley now, have them check for the gun. See if patrol can find any witnesses that might have heard the shots to assist with a timeline, anything will help, and have someone check for a phone. Who walks around in this day and age without a phone?"

Jack walked toward Emma as she spoke nodding his head and writing in his notebook.

She continued, "Have your guys document all these footprints that walk up to the body and back out of the alley. They came after the storm... see if they belong to the boys that reported finding the body, I'll want to talk to them after I read your report."

"I know my job, Detective. My team will document every detail they uncover. If it's here, we'll find it and it will be in the report." His amused expression belied his impressive skills as he took the last few steps toward her.

"You're right, Jack sorry. You're the best."

"Hey! I thought I was the best!" Mitch teased.

Emma shrugged her shoulders, "Your right Mitch, you caught me. Truth is, I think you're both the best... at what you each do, how's that for diplomacy?"

"That's what it's all about, Emma," Jack agreed. "So Mitch, what have you two come up with so far?"

Mitch began speaking while Jack continued taking notes. Emma watched the two of them interact. Jack could only be described as an average looking man. Average height, average weight, average build. But Jack Davis was anything but average. A glance didn't take into account his agile mind and strategic worldview that allowed him to climb the ranks to his present position. He was head of his own crew at just forty-two. Emma knew that under Jack's leadership his unit was already considered one of the best Investigative Support Units in New York state. In her mind, there was no one better suited for that job. She nodded as Mitch continued giving Jack all the information they had gathered, absently watching Jack's pen while he wrote. Emma was confident that his seasoned team really were the best at what they did. Jack's reports were par excellence - always thorough and to the point, thanks in some small way to his OCD which proved to be a plus when collecting all those details. He documented even the tiniest bit of what seemed to be unimportant information that sometimes ended up being pivotal in court. The D.A.s held him in high regard.

When Mitch finished, Emma spoke to Jack. "We're headed for the vic's last known address. Have one of your people find the owner of 441 Meigs Street, apartment 3 and get permission for us to search it. Let me know as soon as you have it. Oh, and when your unit's finished, call animal control about the rats, and waste management to have this alley cleaned out. Thanks Jack."

Emma and Mitch returned to the street, leaving Jack and his men to finish up. They climbed into her police issued Chevy Cruze. She placed the key into the ignition as Mitch punched in the address. While they waited for the GPS to work its magic, she pulled the elastic band out of her long, curly, dark brown hair, twisted it back into a tighter ponytail, and re-pinned it close to her head. Her oval face sported no makeup to highlight her bright blue-green eyes and even though she played down her looks, she was still trim and attractive for her age. She cringed when she checked the mirror and spotted the lines around her eyes. Still she was grateful there were no lines above her lips, a little bonus for not smoking, she assumed. Oh hell, what do you expect, you're 36 years old. Besides, there's a good chance the mirrors are defective on this car. She laughed at herself.

Mitch interrupted her thoughts. "Got it! 441 Meigs Street is just off Monroe Ave. Only five minutes from here." Emma drove to Meigs Street and parked across from 441 while Mitch continued working on his phone. "DMV doesn't have any vehicle registered in the name of Luther Maxwell at this address."

"Could be he took the bus. There are bus stops on the corner." As Emma exited the car, she observed a young couple enjoying the covered porch that graced the front of the converted house. They were sitting on an old couch, smoking and chatting. They stopped to stare when the detectives walked up the stairs toward them. Emma introduced herself and Mitch as they flashed their badges.

Mitch asked if they knew Luther Maxwell.

"Oh sure, detective," said the woman, "he lives in the back apartment, but he's not home."

"We haven't seen him for a few days now. Is he in trouble?" asked the man.

"Do you mind if I record our conversation?" Emma asked.

"I guess not," the woman answered. The man nodded his agreement.

Emma removed the slim, pencil-sized digital recorder from her pocket and clicked it to the ON position. "What is your name, sir?"

"Richard Jones, but my family calls me Rick."

"And where do you live, Rick?"

"441 Meigs Street, Apartment 1"

"Do you know a man by the name of Luther Maxwell?"

"Yes, ma'am."

"Do you know where Luther Maxwell lives?"

"Yes, he lives in the back studio apartment, number 3."

"What can you tell me about Mr. Maxwell, Rick?"

"Well, just that he's quiet, keeps to himself. We don't see him much really."

"That's right," agreed the woman. "He just nods when he sees us. The only reason I know his name is cause it's on the mailbox in the hallway."

"What's your name, ma'am?"

"Debora Jones, but everybody calls me Deb."

"Thank you, Deb."

Rick spoke up again. "He comes and goes at odd hours, so I don't know what kind of job he has, but it must pay well because the landlord told me that he always pays his rent with cash and it's always on time."

"Does he live alone as far as you know?"

"Yes, I'm sure no one lives with him, at least, I've never seen him with anyone," replied Deb.

"So you've never seen him with a friend, girlfriend, relative, co-worker, anyone that might have visited him?"

They shook their heads.

"Please answer verbally," Emma instructed.

"No ma'am," they replied in unison.

"One last question, did he drive a car?"

"No, I never saw him drive. He always took the bus or walked."

Emma thanked them for their time and clicked off the recorder.

"Please feel free to call either one of us if you think of anything else." They extended business cards. Mitch concluded the interview and followed Emma into the foyer. They found several locked mail receptacles and checked Maxwell's mail using one of the keys Emma found on his body.

Mitch thumbed his way through the small collection of paper. "Nothing's in here but junk mail." He replaced the mail, closed and relocked the receptacle. They continued down the hallway to the back apartment. They stood outside the unpainted door with the number 3 hanging upside down and waited.

A few minutes passed before Emma's phone produced a chirp. She pulled it out of her pocket and read the text message out loud. "Jack said the landlord's been contacted, we have permission to enter. He also put in for a warrant, so we're covered in any event." She pushed the key into the lock and gave it a twist. The door opened and they walked into the small studio apartment.

"I've got this," Mitch turned on his recorder. "Luther Maxwell's apartment, 8:55 am. Bare bones for furniture, cheap art, budget lamps… if the guy ever had money he didn't spend it on decor! I don't see any electronics except for that 65-inch TV screen bolted to the wall."

"What's with you guys and your fascination with gigantuous TV screens?"

"I assume that's a rhetorical question." Mitch teased.

They continued to inspect the apartment, poking and prodding, thumbing through the miscellaneous remnants on the coffee and kitchen tables. She heard Mitch open the fridge and call out, "Just a loaf of bread, beer and leftover pizza in the fridge, nothing but vodka and ice cubes in the freezer except for this disgusting frozen sock."

Emma turned to look at Mitch as he removed the object from the freezer.

"Oh, hell," he exclaimed, "it's a Death Wish sock... full of quarters... makes a good billy club. Saw it in an old Charles Bronson movie." Mitch slapped it against his hand before tossing it back into the freezer.

Emma returned to opening and closing drawers, digging through what sparse belongings the man had as they searched everything in the small apartment. "Speaking of weapons, I just found a gun cleaning kit, from the smell, it was used recently. Look at this Mitch, there's a bundle of cash underneath it. So much for being broke. I'll call Jack and have him send a crew over here to document everything and seal this place up."

"Check this out, Emma. This dresser drawer is full of jewelry and wallets with IDs, looks like our victim was a one-man crime spree. Could be one of his victims decided to get even."

Emma was looking at her phone, reading a text, then dropped it back into her jacket pocket. "Jack has a crew on the way. When they get here, we can head back. Find something to carry the wallets, we can start digging through the IDs to see if we can get anything useful. Looks like our suspect pool just got bigger. With any luck, Doc will have discovered something from the DB."

Mitch nodded and started tossing the wallets into a plastic sack he'd found in one of the kitchen drawers. "Can we swing by the donut shop on the way back? I need to pick up something for breakfast. I'm starved! Call came in before I had time to eat this morning."

Emma chuckled to herself. Mitch was like a Labrador... totally food-obsessed. She wondered if he'd run after a tennis ball, better yet, a donut. Her mind instantly created a moving picture of her tossing a donut into the air and Mitch jumping up to catch it in his mouth. "Actually, it's closer to lunchtime and I'm hungry too. Why don't we stop at the diner and get a decent meal instead of that junk food you're always eating?"

"Gee thank you so much Mother Mason. What kind of cop would I be if I didn't love donuts? But if you insist we have something nutritious, I accept. Anything works, as long as I can eat. I'm getting hangry!"

"Hangry! Really Mitch, do you have to bastardize the English language with your amalgams?"

"Why not, everyone knows English is a crazy language, for instance, why do slim chance and fat chance mean the same thing? Or how about if you have some odds and ends, what do you call it when you have just one?"

"You're right Mitch, you need food and fast."

After a quick lunch break they returned to the station and parked in the basement closest to the morgue entrance. They walked through the large double doors that led to the hallway and then into the morgue where they found Doc MacGee eating his lunch off one of the metal examination tables while reading the newspaper. Emma involuntarily shivered at the sight.

"Doc, I'll never understand how you can eat in here with all these bodies."

Doc MacGee just laughed at her discomfort. "They never complain, and I don't have to share. If you grew up with seven brothers and sisters, you would appreciate that."

"I highly doubt that. What have you got for us?"

"So far, I've only had time to send the clothing upstairs to the lab and I sent the bullet to ballistics. I've got my team looking for next of kin. I'll be doing the autopsy after lunch. Anything specific you think I should be looking for?"

"No, just routine. Can you tell if he was right or left handed?"

"I can give you an educated guess from little clues, like which hand his watch was on, the calloused skin found on his writing hand, how his belt was buckled, it's not exactly foolproof, but best guess is he was right handed. Combine that with a sample of his handwriting and you'll be good."

"Thanks, Doc."

Emma shivered as they walked out of the morgue into the warm hallway. "I know that Doc's got the right attitude, but I doubt if I could ever be that comfortable in a room full of bodies."

"That's just life, Emma, or I should say death. If people stopped killing each other, we'd be out of a job."

"Really Mitch, that's how you look at our job?"

"I think it's only commonsensical. Now what do you want me to do next?"

As they rode the elevator up to their floor, Emma asked Mitch to start contacting the people who owned the wallets and draw up a timeline to see how long Maxwell had been working the streets. They were accumulating a lot of circumstantial evidence, but she had a nagging thought in the back of her mind that this case might never be solved. They were missing the gun, the motive and any person of interest. Hell, he might have even killed himself and they were wasting their time investigating a suicide. Oh well, she still had to fill out all the paperwork and start a file on Luther Maxwell regardless of where it would lead. That would take care of the rest of her day. She was glad they had stopped to eat. One or two cups of coffee from the break room would be all she would need to make it through the rest of the day. On second thought, as she remembered how unexceptional the coffee was, she decided it was time to switch to tea. Pretty hard to muck that up.

When she sat down at her desk she opened the bottom drawer that held some files and slid them to the front of the drawer to expose two old tea tins. She lifted them out and opened first one and then the other and smiled when she verified they were both full. One with Oreos and the other with salted peanuts. Sweet and salty save the day once again. She removed 3 cookies and a handful of peanuts to nibble on while she worked.

The next time she looked at the clock it was time to lock up and head for home. Emma looked forward to going home where she could work out to counter the effects of sitting at her desk during the day. She had installed a punching bag and exercise bike, which together, comprised what she referred to as her home gym.

# CHAPTER 3

Emma continued to slam her fist into the punching bag hanging from the exposed beam while she danced around it. She put all her power into every punch. When her muscles began to burn, she slowed her pace. She threw one last punch then began shaking her arms and jogging in place. After wiping sweat from her brow with the small towel at her waist, she walked over to the stationary bike and hopped on to begin her customary 20-mile ride. Her routine was interrupted by a loud thump, thump, thump on her door.

"Who's there?" she hollered in the direction of the door.

"Just me," came the familiar reply.

Emma got off the bike, crossed to the door, unlocked the double locks, threw back the safety slide and opened the door. Her neighbor and best friend, Jean Doyle, blew through the door much like a rogue wave sweeps into the rocky shore, causing an instant disturbance in everything it touches.

"What's up girlfriend?" Emma asked as she climbed back onto her bike. She was determined to keep her focus and complete her routine.

"Just came over to drag you out for some fun."

"What makes you think I'm not having fun right here? I have to stay in shape to catch bad guys, which in my opinion is the most fun a girl can have. I can't tell you how satisfying it is when I see the expression on their faces, when they realize they've been outsmarted and caught. Now that's my idea of FUN."

"Okay. Whatever. I don't have time to argue the merits of our different opinions regarding the meaning of the word. Let me rephrase my question into a factual statement. I would like to go to the Lilac Festival in Highland Park tonight. I want to listen to a new band that's playing. They call themselves, Tommy & the Tremors, I've heard they are really good. Should be a big crowd and great music, we can grab something to eat in one of the food tents. Come on, Em, I really don't want to go alone. It's a warm evening, the lilacs are in full bloom and the entire park smells wonderful, but most important, we haven't had a girls' night out since for-ev-er!" Jean whined and made a pouty face as she exaggerated each syllable of her last word.

"Fine, you convinced me. Let me finish my work out and take a shower. I can be ready to go in an hour, come back then."

"Really! You'll go? Great! You got it. I'll be back in exactly one hour. Don't get off your bike, I can let myself out. Oh, leave your gun and your "*copatude*" home please." Jean hollowered as she swept out the door, slamming it behind her.

"My gun and attitude are always with me," Emma shouted at the closed door. "Deal with it!"

An hour later, Jean was again knocking at her door.

*        *        *

The band was playing by the time Jean parked her car on Goodman Street. They walked into Highland Park carrying their blanket, a tote bag containing snacks and a plastic bottle filled with cranberry juice with a small amount of wine mixed in.

People were everywhere, making their way around the displays and exhibits looking to find that unique gift or treasure to purchase. Emma and Jean walked past the crowds at the tents and made their way toward the music. Emma nodded silent greetings to the uniformed policemen on traffic and security detail keeping watch over the crowd. They didn't have to walk far to reach their destination. They stood on the edge of the lawn that formed a natural amphitheater around the stage. They were looking for any small unoccupied space that they could squeeze into. Emma took advantage of the moment to inhale, filling her lungs with the scent of the lilac bushes combined with the assorted smells coming from the food trucks. The combination blended into the most delicious aroma that permeated the evening air. Jean pointed out a patch of grass big enough to spread out their blanket and they soon settled down to enjoy the warm evening and the rock and roll music being played with uninhibited enthusiasm by the five older men on stage.

Jean walked off to get food while Emma watched the band play. They reminded her of her father and his friends. She focused on the one that was playing the mouth organ, otherwise known as the harmonica. Emma recognized the Beatles song, *Let It Be*. The tune made her a little wistful, as she hummed along. She thought the words were something about finding an answer, *let it be, let it be*. She felt a wave of contentment engulf her as she agreed, in due course, she would find the answers, that was her job. The song switched now to an old Elvis tune, *Jailhouse*

*Rock.* She found the music uplifting but relaxing as well. The musicians looked to be enjoying themselves as much as the people who were watching and listening to them.

Jean interrupted her thoughts when she returned with two plates piled high with food. "Dig in, I couldn't make up my mind so I bought one of each. We can share. My treat."

"Thanks Jean, they smell wonderful. I'm officially off my diet for tonight."

"I knew you would enjoy this. You really do need to get out more."

"You're right. Thanks for the food and I'm so glad you suggested this. It was just what I need after a day of chasing leads that failed to provide answers. Tomorrow is another day."

They relaxed listening to the music while they enjoyed their food and beverages. When Emma was finished eating, she drew her knees up, circled her arms around them, rested her chin on her knees and closed her eyes. Only her foot moved as she tapped her toes, completely relaxed as she listened to the music.

# CHAPTER 4

Jean Doyle was pleased with herself. She had wanted to attend the Lilac festival but hadn't really thought she would be able to entice Emma to join her. Now here they were, enjoying the music, the food, all the wonderful aromas and the fresh air. Only thing missing to her way of thinking was a man. She was surveying the crowd, looking for any single man that might be potential boyfriend material. Jean was three years younger than Emma. She had been married once for a short time but preferred the independence offered by the single life. Truth was, she readily admitted to being a bit of a serial dater, what her mother used to call, 'boy crazy.' She enjoyed her role as a modern, take charge woman. It was a role reversal from the Fifties when her mother grew up. The 21st century allowed her to be free and independent, no longer shackled financially or by society with the limited choices that had restricted the women of her mother's generation. Her friend Emma was a prime example, a decorated police detective who had climbed through the ranks of a male dominated field to become a senior homicide detective. Single women were growing in strength and numbers.

Jean was not embarrassed to be single and on the prowl for a man. She was comfortable taking the lead and making the first move, but then, she also enjoyed the traditional role of being pursued by the smitten suitor. It was like an interesting game to her. Tag, I picked you, now see if you can catch me.

Jean continued to peruse the crowd until she spotted two men standing under a nearby tree. They looked promising. She watched them for a while to see if they were with wives or girlfriends. Thirty minutes passed and they were still standing alone with just an occasional nod to those who walked past. She decided it would be worth walking over to talk to them but she knew Emma would never agree to her approaching complete strangers. Jean had a plan that she had used in the past.

"Emma, I see someone I know over there," she pointed her manicured finger. "Standing under that tree. I'm going over to say hello. I won't be long."

"Fine, I'll be right sitting here enjoying the music till you get back."

Jean stood up with a graceful motion and moved toward the men with confidence. She knew she was considered a "catch" and took slow, deliberate steps with just enough hip movement to ensure their complete attention as she approached. Her long blond hair was perfectly groomed, her makeup expertly applied, and her outfit was selected to show off her exceptional figure to advantage.

She approached the men with a smile on her face, making sure she had their complete attention before she reached them. Then she flashed her friendliest smile while extending her hand in what she imagined was a most delightful fashion. Oh yes, she was an expert at this game.

"Hello, my name is Jean," she offered in the most demure manner she could manage. "Are you two gentlemen here by yourselves?"

"As a matter of fact, we are. I'm so pleased to meet you Jean. I'm Peter Hartman and this is my friend Paul Spears." Peter bowed his head slightly as he accepted her outstretched hand and added, "We are indeed, both single and would be honored if you and your friend would like to join us this evening."

Paul plucked Jean's hand from Peter's to hold in his own as he gazed into her eyes. "*Enchanté*... I'm indeed delighted to make your acquaintance."

Jean feigned a blush, "Seriously? Peter and Paul? That's so adorable! Are you guys waiting for Mary?" She giggled, even as they looked unsure of what to say next.

"Peter, Paul and Mary? The folk trio. Back in the 60's." She continued to get blank looks. "They sang *Puff the Magic Dragon*?" Still nothing. "How about, *I'm Leaving on a Jet Plane*?"

"Oh I've heard that one, they play it on the oldies radio station."

Jean cringed at the reference. "Thank you Paul, you're my savior." Feeling a bit awkward, she decided to change tactics. "Oldies aside, I was just sitting over there with my friend Emma, and she said she would really like to meet you Peter, but she's shy. So I told her I knew you, and I would introduce the two of you. I hope you won't make a liar out of me." Jean turned on the charm, half smiling and half frowning at Peter.

Peter looked in Emma's' direction. "I'm flattered... I confess, I had my eye on her as well." He waved his hand and smiled at Emma.

Jean motioned to Emma to come over and join them. Then turned and moved closer to Paul, using all her best moves as she focused her attention on him like a playful kitten stalking her prey.

Paul leaned in close. "Jean, what say you and I go for a short walk after you introduce them. We could get to know each other. Would you like that?"

"Why you must be reading my mind, Paul. I'm going to have to be careful what I'm thinking when I'm around you."

They both laughed, filled with the feelings of expectation and desire that permeate the beginning of every new relationship.

# CHAPTER 5

Emma saw Jean and Peter waving at her, she smiled and waved back. Then she watched as Jean's wave morphed into a gesture indicating that she wanted Emma to join them.

Great, here we go, she thought to herself, Jean must be on the prowl for a new boyfriend and she wants me to entertain her friend while she scopes out his friend. Well  what the hell, that's what friends do for each other, one "wing woman" coming up.

She reluctantly arose, shrugging her shoulders as she accepted her intrinsic duty assigned by the label BFF. She would take one for the team, but Jean would owe her big time.

"Hello, Emma," Peter extended his hand as she approached, "I'm Jean's friend, Peter. So very pleased to meet you."

"And this handsome gentleman is Paul." Jean added. "Paul and I are going to walk around the park and check out the lilacs while you two keep each other company."

Emma arched her eyebrows. "Whoa girlfriend, wait just one minute, you're talking about over 100 acres of lilac bushes to check out. Where exactly are you headed?" Emma didn't care if she sounded sarcastic with a touch of overprotective parent. "Remember we agreed to stay together when we go out? After all, 'stranger danger' is not just for children. No offense, Paul."

"Oh, it's ok, none taken. I understand. You can't be too careful these days; Peter doesn't let me out of his sight either."

Emma frowned. "Okay, now you're just messing with me."

"Yeah, but I understand, actually I just wanted to walk over to get a beer. We'll be in line at the Genesee beer truck, we won't be far." With that, Jean and Paul turned and headed for the long line of people waiting for the local favorite.

Emma and Peter stood there in uncomfortable silence as they watched them walk away.

"So," Peter broke the silence, "do you like the band?"

"Actually, I think they're pretty good, I like the way the lead singer gets into each song. I'm just guessing, but since the name of the band is Tommy and the Tremors, that must be Tommy.

"That makes sense." Peter fidgeted during another long silence, then asked, "Do you come to Highland park often?"

"No, just for the Lilac Festival." After a brief pause, she added, "Jean wanted to come tonight, she likes to get out during the festival. I'm just keeping her company." The silence continued, Emma felt compelled to resume the dialogue. "Last year Jean talked me into joining her and a few thousand others to shatter the Guinness World Record. It was truly awesome." Emma began to relax as she recalled the experience. "We came here, to the festival, and we were given colored ponchos in shades of purple, pink or green to represent the lilac blossom and the stem. A team of gardeners from Cornell Extension arranged us into the correct shape and they took our picture from overhead. There were 2,297 of us and we formed the world's largest human flower, taking the record away from England. That was quite an experience, in fact, you can still google the picture on the internet." She stopped rambling because Peter was staring at her now. She stammered, "How about you? Do you come to the park often?"

"I don't live far from here, so I do enjoy this park whenever I can. Tonight though, Paul just dragged me out because, well, according to him, I work too much and don't play enough. Truth is, Paul's visiting from Florida, he's between girlfriends and he didn't want to come here and listen to the music by himself."

"That's funny, we have almost the same story. I didn't mind though; I do enjoy this festival. Listening to the music, watching the people, the food, the smells, how about you?"

"I used to come here with my girlfriend to enjoy the flowers and people watch, but since she died last year, it just makes me sad. I look around and see happy couples, walking hand in hand, enjoying the evening and the music together. I guess the truth is, I'm jealous because they seem so happy. Sharing the evening, their lives, with someone they love."

"Oh, don't let them fool you. You know what they say about behind closed doors."

"Yeah, I certainly know a thing or two about that, but just the same, I was wishing I had someone to hold hands with while we strolled together through the park."

"Well," Emma smiled as her playful side took over, "come on then." She grabbed Peter's hand and started to pull him toward the sidewalk that circled the bandstand and wound around the perimeter of the concert area.

"Wait, what are you doing? Where are you going?" Peter followed alongside her looking very awkward and unsure of himself.

"I thought I would make your wish come true." Emma stated. Her high spirits and good humor only encouraged by the awkwardness and discomfort he was displaying.

"Oh great! If I knew you were going to grant my wish, I'm sure I could think of something else I would much rather have wished for. I don't suppose I can get a do over if I say please?"

Emma laughed out loud at his quick wit and sense of humor. She could appreciate that he didn't take himself too seriously.

"Sorry, no do overs today. I gave them all away and I won't have any more until tomorrow." Emma laughed.

Peter smiled back at her. "You have a wonderful laugh. I bet you really enjoy life."

"I'll take that bet. My favorite quote is from Oscar Wilde who said; *'Life is too important to be taken seriously'*."

"I would have to agree with Mr. Wilde, most of the time."

"We have to tell Jean and Paul what we are doing so they won't worry."

They walked hand in hand to the beer truck then spent the next twenty minutes listening to the music while they walked and talked about nothing in particular. When they completed the circle and returned to the tree where they had met, Jean and Paul were standing there listening to the music. Emma noticed that

Jean was not flirting and seemed uninterested in further conversation with Paul.

"Well, guys" Jean stated as soon as Emma and Peter rejoined them, "it was really nice talking with you, but we've taken up enough of your time. Nice seeing you again, Peter. Goodbye Paul."

Emma hesitated, then followed Jean.

Peter called out as they walked away. "Wait, Emma, I don't even know your last name!"

"It's Mason, like in Perry Mason, only I'm a cop, not a lawyer."

Emma knew from past experience that, more often than not, once a man found out she was a cop, he lost interest in her as a potential date, much less girlfriend material. Too bad, she did like Peter but now that he knew what she did for a living she did not expect to hear from him again. Emma seldom told people her occupation when she first met them in social situations. People became uncomfortable when they learn you enforce the law for a living. She often wondered how an IRS agent or a funeral director handled that same situation. She smiled when she heard Tommy & the Tremors began to play Bobby Darin's hit, *If I was a Carpenter*. How appropriate she thought.

Once they were settled again on their blanket, drinks in hand, Emma's curiosity got the best of her. "So Jean, that was a record even for you. What happened with your handsome Prince Charming?"

"OMG, that guy's the last of the chauvinistic pigs, a throwback to the Neanderthals, in fact, his name should be NeanderPaul."

"Wow, that's strong, even for you, what the hell happened?" Emma was amused, in spite of her genuine concern at her friends distress.

"Well we were barely in line when he asked me if I had ever considered having a boob job. Do you believe it? Me? Fake boobs?" She pulled her shoulders back and heaved her chest out to emphasize how perfect they were. "He said he liked big boobs and only dated women who had double D's or larger. I asked him if he dated much and he said I would be surprised at how many women were only too happy to accommodate him. Most women, according to him, want bigger boobs and he just helps them get what they already want. He said if I was interested in having a boob job, he would pay for it, no strings attached. I couldn't believe it! I was speechless! I didn't know what to say."

"Knowing you, I'm sure that didn't last long before you thought of something. What, pray tell, did you say?"

Jean smiled with satisfaction. "I told him I might consider it if he would have his legs stretched since I preferred to date taller men. Then I thought about it and added that he would also have to consider a brain transplant because I am bored by primitive thinking men."

"Oh, snap! You are good!" Emma admired Jean's aptitude at expressing herself with words, probably why her newspaper column was so successful.

"Not to rain on your parade Jean, but I just read that 5% of women in the US have had breast implants, over 300,000 last year alone!"

"But... why would they?"

"Lots of different reasons, I'm sure, but from my professional point of view, it sure helps us identify bodies. Manufactured body parts like knees, hips, metal plates, even silicone implants each have their own individual serial number. We often use them to verify and sometimes even identify our DB."

Jean shuddered. "Well, nobody is ever going to pull serial numbers off my boobs! What a douche he turned out to be, just goes to show good looks aren't everything. I guess that's the last we'll hear from them."

"Too bad, Peter seemed nice. Where do you know him from?"

"Oh, yeah, about that. I didn't actually know him, just said I did so you wouldn't stop me. Sorry for the subterfuge. Forgive me?

"Good God, Jean, you're incorrigible!"

"Peter did seem like a nice guy Em, but you have to wonder about him, judging from his choice of friends. Birds of a feather and all that."

"You're right, our choice of friends does reveal a lot about us. For instance, we hang out together because, well, hmmn, now that I think about it, it's not because we have a lot in common. You love to cook, you enjoy writing, you love going out and socializing. I don't like anything domestic, I enjoy working out and I cherish my time alone. In reality, now that I think about it, we have very little in common!"

"Truth is Em, being your friend is one of the longest relationships I've ever had outside of family. How long has it been? Six, seven years? Ever since you bought the condo across the hall from me."

"Bought it in 2009. But I'm surprised at you, I still have friends that I knew in childhood and high school. I believe in the song I learned in the brownie's, *make new friends, but keep the old, one is silver and the other's gold.*"

"I'll bet they are all females."

"Come to think of it, most of them are, but there are a few guys in the mix."

"All relationships are hard work, but when it's with the opposite sex, I've found those are the most difficult to navigate and that's if you're lucky enough to find a decent man to make it worth all the effort." Jean added.

Emma laughed as her mind flashed back over her last few disastrous pairings. "I admit I haven't had much luck with my choices. Thank God I have a job that I love. I really don't have time for dating anyway. I don't know how you find time to date with your full time job plus writing your advice, slash, lovelorn column for the newspaper!"

"Where do you think I get all my material from? Now I have at least two interesting and controversial columns for next month, thanks to Paul. Even without the column though, I enjoy having a man in my life. Not to marry, I'll never do that again! But dating is always an interesting experience that I never get tired of. I enjoy meeting new people and the entire concept of dating in general. You learn something new from everyone you date. I learned how to downhill snow ski and sail from Joe K."

Emma signed, "You're right! I learned how to scuba dive when I dated Sal, he was on the police water search and rescue team. I really enjoyed our vacation on that dive boat cruising around the Virgin Islands. That was really awesome, diving into the beautiful, clear waters of the Caribbean. We even did a night dive; it was an amazing experience."

"I remember Sal, you told me your nickname for him was Salvadorable. Cute. What happened with him, he sounded perfect."

"Well like I told him, he wasn't perfect, but I thought he was perfect for me. Trouble was his daughters weren't ready to share. Too much drama for me to overcome."

"When you moved in next door to me, you were dating Jerry. Didn't he teach you how to ballroom dance?

"Truth is, we learned together, he was a very good dancer, made me look good. I do miss dancing with him and it was a fun way to exercise and stay in shape."

"I still remember you guys at Sandra's wedding, everyone was admiring how the two of you danced to the Swing music from the 40's."

"My favorite dance was the Cha Cha, and he was very good at inventing new moves that looked great on the dancefloor."

"They say good moves on the dance floor means good moves in bed." Jean teased.

"I'll never tell, Emma replied.

"Oh, how about when you fixed me up with your cousin John, the air traffic controller. He taught me how to golf and waterski. Losing his leg, when he served in Vietnam didn't slow him down one bit. I think about him and all the fun we had together, until he moved to Arkansas that is."

"Didn't you go down and visit him once after he moved?"

"Yes, and it was awesome, we went golfing with his friends, they were so nice and hospitable. John is very happy there."

"I remember he would tell me that he liked the way you, as he put it, 'trimmed his antlers'!"

They enjoyed a hearty laugh about that, until people around them started shushing them.

"Thanks Jean, for getting me to come out tonight, it was fun and you were right, I do need to go out more in order to appreciate the good in people. I see so much of the bad in my job, it's important to even it out so I can stay balanced."

They continued talking and enjoying the evening until the music ended. It was growing dark when they gathered up their belongings and headed home.

Strange how they never ran out of things to talk about… never experienced the uncomfortable silences that sometimes invaded the conversations between herself and her dates. Perhaps it was because girlfriends shared, they didn't judge. They understood and sympathized, they didn't try to force solutions. Reminded her of her well-read book by John Gray, titled, *Men are from Mars, Women are from Venus.* Now that's a man who knows what he's talking about.

## CHAPTER 6

The next morning, Emma felt energized as she walked into the lobby holding a cup of her favorite gourmet coffee from the coffee shop around the corner. The one small luxury she sometimes allowed herself. She continued up the stairs to her floor and nodded to the few officers still finishing up reports from the night shift. She smiled when she arrived at her office and noticed the distinctive green envelope from ballistics waiting in her inbox. Setting her coffee down and ripping open the sealed envelope, she skimmed over the report. Emma rang Mitch and asked him to come to her office so they could go over it together.

"Well, you look rested this morning," Mitch observed as he walked in, sipping coffee and eating a chocolate covered donut. "Do something interesting last night?"

Emma gazed with longing at the donut in Mitch's hands.

She loved donuts, but they were a treat she seldom allowed herself. "Jean and I went to the Lilac Festival to listen to a concert. It was a perfect evening, the music was right on, a great new band, you would like them, Tommy and the Tremors. They drew a huge crowd, I heard they broke another attendance record. In spite of all the people, everybody was relaxed and enjoying themselves. We ended up having a pleasant evening and the lilacs were amazing, as always."

"Amanda loves the Lilac festival. She enjoys talking to the artists and looking at all the original crafts and artwork on display. I like to walk around the Vietnam memorial garden. Something in the park for everyone."

"Speaking of Amanda begs the question, are you guys back together?"

"No. At least I don't think so. She called and invited me to walk around the festival grounds over the weekend. It's only two blocks from her apartment and she wanted company. Our relationship always seems like a work in progress - more like friends with benefits. She's a very complicated lady, and I don't even want to get into what her family is like but dysfunctional is the name of their family tree." He laughed at his own joke, took a breath and added, "they put the FUN in dysfunctional."

Emma just smiled and shook her head. He noticed the report in her hand as he shoved the last of the donut into his mouth. "So, what did we get from ballistics?"

"Right! Back to work. So, according to this report, the bullet that killed Luther Maxwell matched a gun that was connected to a number of unsolved cases. Chronologically, from the most recent event, this same gun was used to kill a 22-year-old college co-ed named Colleen Marks. A 46-year-old man named George Tyler. An ATM robbery where the 34-year-old male victim, name of Red Lemcke fought back. He survived but was shot in the leg. The robbery of a gas station on the northeast side, bullet found in the ceiling. All unsolved. Then it seems there was a period of 6 years before that with no reported activity and a spate of gang related shootings on the southeast side of the city in the years before that."

"Wow, that's impressive, we got all that overnight, how many people work in the ballistics unit?"

"Not as many as you're thinking. They sent it through that new computer program DA-FIST, developed by the digital analysis and forensics investigative services team."

"Oh, DA-FIST, gotta love that acronym. So it looks into all the unsolved cases we have and flags any cases involving the same gun by using the bullet Doc MacGee pulled out of Maxwell?"

"Close. From what I understand, it goes through every case, solved or unsolved that involves useable, recovered shell casings and bullets. Everything is entered into the system by type and the striations are all uploaded into the databases. It then flags all cases that match the criteria selected. It's an ongoing program, working with police departments all over the country to expand their database. They're inputting as much available data as possible. I understand some of the bigger cities have dedicated entire units to inputting data. In due course, this program will be able to connect all criminal activity anywhere in the country using any matching criteria that we choose. The days of criminals moving from one state to another to start over clean will soon be history."

"Makes you wonder when computers will be taking over our jobs. Do you worry about that? We could soon be as obsolete as manual typewriters and carbon paper."

"I'm not worried, we still have to investigate the crimes, collect the data that goes into the system and make the arrests, but I do appreciate how much work that program saved us, it would've taken us weeks to connect all this information just a year ago. Now we already have four case files to check out.

You can work the Lemcke file first, he was shot in the leg. See if Mr. Lemcke gave us a composite of the shooter. Maybe we'll get something to work with there. According to this report, looks like the gun wasn't used between 16 and 22 years ago for a period of 6 years. Could be the owner was in prison during that time."

"Or moved to another city. Couldn't have been Maxwell… he would have been too young during the gang shootings."

"You're right, he would have been eight or nine years old when the gun disappeared. Don't think he would have been toting a gun at that age."

"Or been a gang member, not yet anyway, they usually wait till they are at least tall enough to ride the old wooden roller coaster at Sea Breeze Park."

"It's just another unknown piece of the puzzle for now, one step forward, two steps back, that's our job description Mitch. You work those old files and I'll check with Doc and Jack to see what they've uncovered."

I'm on it!" Mitch closed his notebook, picked up his empty coffee cup and walked out.

Emma called Doc MacGee first, and found out that his office had located Luther Maxwell's mother and made arrangements for her to come to the morgue at 2 that afternoon to identify the body and submit a claim for the body. Emma could interview her then.

Emma walked up to Jack's office to see what his unit had. Jack was on the phone when Emma walked in. He had his report all ready and handed it to her while he continued his phone conversation. "That's all well and good sweetheart, but I really don't think we need a second dog." He paused, put his hand over the phone and whispered to Emma, "be just a minute, family crisis." He removed his hand, "since when do each of the kids need to have their own dog? Who's going to end up taking care of them? Not the kids! You know that!" He paused again to listen, then continued, "Fine, fine, I'll think about it. We'll talk about it when I get home. Love you." He hung up the phone and smiled at Emma. "I'll bet you twenty dollars right now that she's already adopted another dog from the rescue kennel. I thought her getting a job there was a good idea, now I can see how this could go sideways on me."

Emma laughed, she liked Jack's wife. "No bet, I only put my money on a sure thing, therefore I'd never bet against Anne. So, what have you got on the Luther Maxwell case?"

"It's all in the report I handed you. At the scene, there were four sets of footprints around the body that were left after the storm. Any footprints before or during the storm were washed away. Two sets matched the boys who found the body and called it in. They swear that they didn't touch anything and they didn't see a gun when they found the body. Their footprints back up their statements. The other two sets are unaccounted for, but it looks like they walked all over the scene and moved the body. If there was a gun or money in his wallet, they certainly could have helped themselves."

"How about the apartment?"

"There again, more questions than answers, we think Maxwell must've owned a gun, you found the cleaning kit. We uncovered several boxes of .38 ammo, but didn't find a gun. He had cash hidden all over the place - secret panels in the closet, hollowed out books, even in the oven, totaled over $17,000 so far. He had two hollowed out phone books, but no phone according to the phone company. I have the apartment sealed off and guarded until we finish. I assigned a fresh unit and they will be tearing the whole place apart today. I expect they will find more hidden cash. We also found more wallets and jewelry, along with a drawer full of pawn tickets from all over town.

Looks like he was a very busy thief. It'll take us weeks to track down all his victims, but I'm confident we'll be able to close out dozens of open cases and eventually return the stolen property to the rightful owners. At least with the perpetrator dead, we don't have to hold on to their property as evidence until after the trial. I'm thinking that your killer did everyone a favor on this one."

"Yeah, God forbid, I was thinking the same thing, and I'm beginning to think he may have used Maxwell's own gun to do it, or maybe Maxwell wasn't his first kill and now he's got another gun for his collection. More loose ends we need to tie together as we find answers."

"Always the chance he shot himself and the gun was stolen after the fact. The gloves he was wearing did test positive for gunpowder."

"Right, we haven't ruled out suicide. Have you found anything that indicated whether Maxwell was right or left handed?"

"Yeah. We found handwriting samples at the apartment. Appears he was right handed. I got something interesting from his rap sheet. Turns out he was on trial just two weeks ago for a break-in on Monroe Avenue in March. The residents saw him running out the back door of their apartment when they returned from shopping. They called 911 and patrol was on scene within the hour. They traced footsteps in the snow from the crime scene right up to Maxwell's back porch where they recovered the stolen purse, contents dumped out and cash missing. They were familiar with Maxwell, so as they drove around the neighborhood they watched for him. When they spotted him walking down the street, they stopped him and brought him in for questioning.

He claimed he found the purse on his back porch and was walking to the police station to turn in the money he found inside. When the officers asked him why just the cash, he replied that he had a reputation to protect and couldn't be seen in his neighborhood carrying a purse."

Jack paused to glance at Emma's reaction before he continued. She smiled at Maxwell's comment. Jack continued reading. "At the trial, Maxwell produced an alibi. A Mr. Ronald Reed, who claimed to be a friend. He testified that they were sitting in his truck drinking when the crime was committed. The judge didn't believe any of it, but reasonable doubt existed and he had to let him go. Maxwell walked out of court almost two weeks ago."

"That is interesting. Reasonable doubt sometimes puts an unreasonable twist to our justice system. Do we have an address on this Mr. Reed? I'd like to see what he has to say now that his friend is dead."

"It's all in the report." Jack replied as his phone rang and he reached to pick it up. He nodded at Emma as she rose to leave his office.

Emma bounded down the two flights of stairs between her floor and Jack's, through the fire door and down the hall to her office. She glanced out the window as she entered. The sun was out in full force. A bright, sunny day in Rochester. Emma was pleased with her new office, but especially with the window that came with it. Even though she was on the first floor, the building was designed so her floor was one level up from the lobby. That made it high enough to allow the sun to shine in every day. That is, every day the sun came out, after all, she did live in Rochester, New York. Currently it held the undesirable position of the sixth cloudiest city of its size in the United States. It was a title many Rochesterians' were proud of but most just endured by repeating the mantra, 'if you don't like the weather, wait five minutes'.

She moved into this office just a month ago from one of the smaller, windowless offices in the center of the building. She was still amazed that she now had her own office with a window. The

Detective Sergeant had told her it was because of all her hard work, but she knew she had been next in line to inherit this office when Detective O'Reilly retired. Seniority is everything when they're handing out the keys to the offices in the police department. She knew the truth. It was her turn. It only took her 15 years but here she was, standing in an office with a window and the sun was shining brightly through it. Oh happy day!

She fought her desire to daydream and forced herself to concentrate. She was soon absorbed in organizing her murder board and sketching out the timeline. As usual, she worked through her lunch, but found a protein bar in her purse. A cup of coffee and a handful or two of salty peanuts would be all she needed.

# CHAPTER 7

At 2 o'clock Emma entered the morgue to witness the identification of Luther Maxwell by his mother. Emma heard her before she saw her - half sobbing and half yelling at Doc MacGee about how badly she was always being treated and how unfair life was for her. When Emma entered the room, Mrs. Maxwell turned her attention on her, crossed the room and wrapped her arms around Emma's shoulders, crying in loud, dramatic sobs.

Emma flinched, but stood her ground. Not only did she not appreciate being hugged by this stranger, but the familiar odor of formaldehyde was being overpowered by the body odor coming from the woman hugging her. Doc MacGee was standing next to the viewing window with his arms folded, watching the performance.

Wow, thought Emma, what has she got against hygiene? Her unkempt appearance and aversion to bathing reminded her of Eliza Doolittle, before her first bath, in *My Fair Lady*.

Emma heard Doc MacGee clear his throat, then, in his most professional demeanor he continued to repeat his question. "Mrs. Maxwell, we need you to officially identify the body. Could you please answer my question? Is this the body of your son, Luther Maxwell?"

"Well, I'd hafta take another look at 'im, it's been awhile, ya know, don't ya? A boy only needs his ma till he hits his teens." She took her time moving back over to the viewing window and looked thru it to the table where the body lay. Doc had a clean sheet covering everything but Luther's head.

Emma looked through the window and noted the excellent job Doc had done repairing the damage from the rats. She watched as Mrs. Maxwell, touched the window that separated her from the body, then looked at the Doctor and asked, "What do I get if this here is my boy? Is there a re-ward? Do I get money fer... you know... so as I can bury him? I'm not a rich woman ya know. Life has not treated me fair, I have the kids, but not the husband." She began to sob again, then took a deep breath, "I get by usin' my wits. I got more at home that need ta eat. I hafta think of them ya know, don't ya?"

Mrs. Maxwell wrapped her arms around herself and pushed her shoulders back while standing as tall as she could. Her look at Doc MacGee was more a challenge than an invitation, as she waited for him to answer her questions.

"I am very sorry for your loss Mrs. Maxwell but I cannot promise you anything in return for your identification. However, if this is your son, the Public Administrator's office will be in touch with you to offer options including help with cost. If you do not choose to claim the body, the county will bury him at no expense to you."

"Will I be able ta visit him if you pay ta bury him?"

Emma stepped in now and introduced herself. She explained to Mrs. Maxwell that she could give her the phone numbers of victim support groups that might be of assistance to her if this was indeed her son. She reassured her that the Public Administrator's Office would work with her to determine her son's final resting place so she could visit, even though Emma was sure she never would.

"Oh, alright then. Ya, that's him, that's my boy, Luther John was his name, named after my father." After a thoughtful hesitation she continued, "He was a good boy, never forgot his Ma, dropped off cash every week or so. He was my oldest what lived, I was 16 when he was born. He never hurt anyone mind ya, do ya know who done it, who killed my boy? He was a good boy." she repeated sadly.

"Did Luther own a gun?"

"O ya, he did! Was right proud of it too. He always had it on him. Ever since he found it on the roof about 10...15 years ago. I'm not good with time." She began to sob again, "He would hav' been comin' over soon with money for me, he always had money to help his por mama."

She became thoughtful, then her mood became hostile. "Say. What happened to all his money? All his stuff? I should get it! He woulda wanted me to have everythin'. Where's it at? Can you tell me where he lived so's I can go there and collect my stuff?"

"I am very sorry for your loss, Mrs. Maxwell, but we are still in the process of collecting and documenting everything found in your son's possession. It's all being held as evidence at this time. It will be a while before we will know more, but I'll be happy to update you after we close the case. Now if you go back to the front desk and ask the clerk for the victim assistance information, he will give you a packet that will help you. Thank you for your cooperation and coming in today Mrs. Maxwell."

"Wait! Now you hold on lady officer. Don't you be hustling me!" The Doc here said he'd get me home. I got kids waitin', I need that ride he promised."

"I'm sorry, of course we can arrange transportation for you. Here's my card, just tell the desk clerk that I said to also make sure you get home safely. He will take care of the arrangements and thank you again for coming in Mrs. Maxwell."

Emma closed the door as soon as Mrs. Maxwell had exited into the hallway. She rolled her eyes and shook her head as she gazed around the room. "Wow Doc, that was really sad. I forget how desperate people become in order to survive in their world. I hope she gets some help. If she was 16 when he was born, then she's only 47 now. Life has not been kind. She looks 10 - 15 years older, poor thing. Did you find anything unusual during the autopsy?"

"No, it was routine. He had a peanut butter and jelly sandwich with a slice of pizza and a couple of beers for his last meal, maybe two hours before he was shot. T.O.D. was 6 days ago, between 5 to 11 pm, just about the time the storm hit. No bruising on his body, nothing to indicate a struggle with his killer. C.O.D. was single 38 caliber bullet directly into the heart."

"Doc, is it possible that he shot himself?"

"It's possible, but not likely. It's just my opinion, based on several things, like where he was found. Most suicides kill themselves in a place that has meaning to them or where their body will be found as soon as possible. I would surmise, from what his mother said, that they were close. He knew that she depended on the money he gave her. I think he would have provided for her before he killed himself. Also, shooting yourself in the heart is very uncommon. Most suicides, if they use a gun, shoot themselves in the head. No, my experience would suggest that Maxwell was murdered by someone he trusted. Death Certificate will say he died under suspicious circumstances for now."

"O.K. Thanks Doc. How's the family?"

"Everyone is fine, thanks for asking. Oh, Jenny, our daughter just told us we're going to be grandparents in 6 months. How about that!"

"Congratulations, you'll make an awesome grandpa."

A silly grin appeared on Doc's face and Emma knew that her statement was right on target.

"Carole is thrilled beyond belief. She's so excited about becoming a grandma that she's already buying baby things. She's going to be taking care of the baby during the day so she's turning our junk room into a nursery. Hand painting the walls with colorful bubbles and blocks floating up to the ceiling and we don't even know if it's a boy or girl yet."

"They should be able to tell by now, shouldn't they?"

"Sure, sure, but Jenny and John don't want to know yet. I don't understand, they say they want it to be a surprise, but I say that the instant you find out, that's when you're surprised. Makes sense to me to be surprised sooner rather than later but you know kids, they have to blaze their own trails."

"Tell your family I said congratulations and best wishes."

Emma was thinking about the innocence of newborn babies as she walked out into the hallway and back to her office. The rest of the day was business as usual. Emma brought Mitch up to speed on the interview with Maxwell's mother. About her statement that Luther found the gun on the roof 10 to 15 years ago. That fit the timeline they had.

Mitch and Emma interviewed the boys that found the body and were satisfied that they didn't know any more than what was already in the report. They went over the statements obtained by patrol when they canvassed the neighbors, hoping someone may have heard the shot now that they had a better idea of when the shooting occurred, but again, they had nothing new. No one heard the shot. The only thing left was to match the wallets and personal property recovered at Maxwell's apartment to the owners and interview them one more time. Jack's unit was working with robbery to handle that.

"At least that will be a positive outcome for a lot of people when they are reunited with their property as a result of this investigation," Emma commented to Mitch.

"I know what you mean, this is one of those times that the world is better off without this guy. I guess it's pretty dismal when you put it into words."

"Anything on that ATM robbery?"

"I've got the complete file right here. Mr. Lemcke did produce a sketch for us to work with." Mitch unfolded the composite sketch from the folder and spread it out on Emma's desk. They both agreed that the composite the victim had supplied looked a lot like Maxwell. Mitch told Emma he had arranged a face to face interview with Mr. Lemcke to see if he could positively identify Maxwell as his assailant. Mr. Lemcke would be there in the morning.

Emma nodded and added that after that interview they were going to visit Mr. Reed to see if he had anything new to add regarding Maxwell's alibi for the robbery in March. It would be interesting to see what Reed had to say now that Maxwell was dead. So far, Reed was the only person Maxwell seemed to trust. At this point in their investigation, he was also their only person of interest.

They were summing up the results of their work when there was a knock at the door. She looked at the clock, it was after four. She got up from her desk to open the door. Brigham, the front desk clerk was standing there holding a large floral arrangement that included several brightly colored balloons that were hovering over his head. Emma glanced behind the clerk, and saw the office staff watching. Brig smiled broadly as he informed her that these had just arrived for Miss Emma Mason. He handed the arrangement to her then departed.

Emma took the flowers and balloons into her office and glanced at her partner. Mitch wasn't even trying to hide his enjoyment at her expense.

"Flowloons for the lady? Did I forget an important date? Is it your birthday today, what's the special occasion?"

"You're enjoying this way too much Detective Delaney, did you do this? Is this your idea?"

"No ma'am, these aren't from me."

"Then I don't know what these are for. Who on earth could they be from?"

When she found the card, her mouth fell open as she read the words;

**Would you grant a second wish and have dinner**

**with me this weekend?    Sincerely, Peter**

Mitch continued to tease, "So, give me a clue. Who sent the bouquet? A secret admirer?"

"No, not secret, just a guy I met last night at the festival. Thing is, I don't know how he knew where to send these, I never gave him anything but my name."

"Well what's his name, I'll run it and check him out for you."

"No thank you, for one, it's none of your business, and two, I don't know his last name."

"I'm sure I don't have to warn you to be careful of men who come on too strong, not a good sign, and why don't you know his last name? He obviously knows yours."

"Enough said, we need to get back to work so we can finish this and call it a day."

"Sure, let's do that, I'm meeting Amanda for dinner and movie night at her place. My turn to pick out the movie at Redbox so I'm looking forward to it."

They added the new information to the board and updated the computer. Emma was satisfied with their progress and was grateful when they had completed everything and Mitch left for his office without mentioning the flowers and balloons she had setting in the corner.

## CHAPTER 8

When it was time to go home, she picked up her purse and briefcase. She was tempted to leave the arrangement and walk out. She was aware of all the eyes that would be watching her as she walked to the elevator. She shrugged her shoulders, picked up the arrangement and walked to the elevator. A co-worker held the doors for her while she struggled to get the flowers and balloons inside before the doors closed. She was parked in the underground garage and was thankful when the elevator doors opened on her floor and a quick glance assured her that it was empty of further spectators.

She struggled again getting all the balloons out of the elevator and into her car. She had to put the flowers on the ground while she shoved the balloons into her back seat, one at a time. She thought she succeeded when she pushed the last one in, only to watch in dismay as one of them floated back out and up to the ceiling. She quickly picked up the flowers and set them on the floor of the back seat with her right hand while shutting the door with her left. She took a minute to regain her composure then opened the driver's door just enough to allow room to squeeze her body into the car. The balloons were floating around her head now, bumping into each other as they bobbed to and fro, obstructing her view. She was losing patience when she spotted grandmother's hat pin in her visor. Grandmother had given it to her years ago, telling Emma that in her day a sturdy hat pin was the only weapon a lady needed. Emma pulled it out of her visor and started attacking the balloons with great delight, until only two survived. Those she tied down so they could not get in her way while she drove home. There, that should do it, she decided, with a silent 'Thank You' to grandma as she replaced the hat pin into her visor. She looked around and saw two older ladies staring at her. She smiled and waved to them, then pulled her car out and drove away.

As she headed home, she thought about Peter and wondered why was he interested in her, why did he send her flowers, why so many damn balloons, why did he not include a way for her to contact him with an answer. Who was he anyway? Emma couldn't wait to tell Jean and get her two cents worth. She turned on the radio and smiled when, *On my Mind* began to play.

Emma had her hands full as she entered the lobby of her multi-story condominium building. Ignoring the elevator, she struggled up the stairs with her briefcase, purse and flowers, along with the two surviving balloons. She always climbed the stairs to her second floor condo two at a time and she was determined that today would be no different. When she arrived on her floor, she set everything down in front of her door so she could unlock the two deadbolts. The door across the hall from hers opened a crack and Jean peeked out.

"Hey, Em, thought I heard you! You're home on time for a change. What have you got there? Whoa, who sent you flowers? Did I forget your birthday? No, that's in March. What are the flowers for? Something happen at work? Did you win something? Are they for you or are you giving them to someone?

"Whoa, slow down girl! At least let me get inside before the interrogation begins."

Jean stepped into the hallway closing and locking her door behind her. She picked up Emma's briefcase and purse as Emma lifted the flowers and balloons. Together they walked into Emma's condo and set everything down on the countertop that divided her kitchen from the dining room.

Emma released the balloons and watched them float up to the kitchen ceiling. Her kitchen was painted a soft, warm yellow with old-fashioned white lace curtains framing the two small windows over the sink. The adjoining walls of the dining and living room were painted in soft tones of green, accented with touches of brightly colored pillows. The pictures that hung on the walls, featured bygone days. Depicting ladies and children strolling through garden settings in their long gowns, carrying lace umbrellas, all in the distinctive oval frames popular in those days. It was an eclectic style that managed to appear organized and comfortable.

They often sat at the kitchen counter to chat and catch up on the day's events or plan new ones.

"So, girlfriend." Jean said as soon as she sat down, her curiosity out of control. "Who sent the balloons and flowers? What's the occasion? Professional or personal?"

"Hold on while I get us something to drink, would you like lemonade or tea?"

"Lemonade sounds good. Answer my questions please. I'm literally dying of curiosity."

"No you're not! You're a writer for God's sake, you're NOT literally dying, at least not from curiosity." Emma slipped the card out and handed it to Jean.

She read it out loud, then jumped off her chair. "Peter! Peter from the festival?" Jean raised her hands in the air and waved them about as she swiveled her hips. "Hot damn girlfriend, you got it goin' on!" she declared laughing.

Then just as suddenly, she stopped dancing and frowned. "Wait, you gave him your address? That's not like you Em, I thought you never gave out your address. You told me yourself cops keep their personal information hidden from the public for a reason."

"We do, and I didn't give him any personal information except that I was single, I was a cop and my name. I don't know how he found out where I work. I thought maybe you told Paul."

"Me? Never, Em! I would never do that. I know how dangerous that could be. How on earth did he find you? And more important, what are you going to do about it? Are you going to see him again? Are you going to make his wish come true?" Jean's smiled as she emphasized each word. "He's got style; you have to give him points for that."

"Honestly, I'm not sure how I feel about any of this. I don't know how he found me first of all, and I'm not sure if it's flattering or just creepy. Plus, I have no way of getting in touch with him even if I did want to see him again. There's no contact information and I don't even know his last name, much less what he does for a living. He just said he was self-employed, that could mean pretty much anything."

"Ah ha, and so the mystery deepens. Anyone here know a smart cop that could help us crack the..." Jean paused here while she made air quotes with her fingers, "case of the elusive admirer? Another in the series of Detective Emma Mason Mysteries!"

"Oh for God's sake, Jean, stop with the dramatics. You're not one bit funny. I'm sure there must be a simple explanation. He must know someone who knows who I am, mystery solved."

"Okay, I'll be serious. Did you read my column about men who stalk women? They surprise them with what seem to be thoughtful gifts and cards and they do and say all the right stuff that women love, give off all the right signals, but underneath, they hate women and only behave that way until they have gained control over them."

"I always read your column, but really Jean, between you and Mitch, I feel like I have another set of parents hovering over me. When did I become a child that had to be protected? I am perfectly capable of taking care of myself. I am armed, remember?"

"And dangerous, you forgot that part. I think men in general are helpless to resist women who are dangerous and mysterious."

"Not to change the subject, but I forgot to eat lunch today and I'm really hungry. I'm going to walk down to the corner and pick up something at Mickey D's, want to come?"

"No thanks, I made supper for both of us. That's why I was waiting for you to come home. I'm experimenting in the kitchen again. I threw together a new concoction and I want an unbiased opinion on whether it's any good.

"What is it this time?" Emma was already anticipating the delicious meal just steps away.

"So happy you asked. First of all, this morning, I put a layer of sauerkraut on the bottom of my crock pot, then added chunks of uncooked pork, carrots and fresh mushrooms, covered it with a final layer of sauerkraut, added a little more liquid, turned it on low and went to work. When I got home, I made fresh mashed potatoes, added a raw egg and I am going to fry the potato mixture in a bit of oil to brown the edges just before serving. Then I'll put the potatoes on the plate and scoop the sauerkraut mixture out of the crock pot and spread it over the potatoes. How does that sound?"

"Sounds wonderful! Now I'm glad I forgot lunch. I really enjoy your cooking. Isn't it funny how different we are, I'm just not interested in cooking, I use my oven for storage. Thank God for the microwave, and frozen foods. Just let me put some water in this vase and change out of my work clothes into something more comfortable and I'll be right over. I'm hungry and in the mood to try something new."

"Terrific, see you in a few." Jean said as she left Emma's.

When Emma walked into Jean's condo, the smell of pork and sauerkraut permeated the air.

"Smells wonderful Jean. I brought a jar of applesauce as my contribution to our meal."

"Thanks, that works. I hope dinner tastes as good as it smells, it was so easy to make, I do love comfort food cooked in my crock pot. Have a seat, pop open the applesauce. Here's a spoon. Dinner will be ready in a few."

Emma looked at the kitchen table and saw that Jean had set the places. "Anything I can do before I sit down?"

"No, just give me an honest opinion of dinner, that's it."

"I'll try, but I do love pork and sauerkraut so I already know I'll love it."

Emma glanced around Jean's condo with its colorful walls and accessories. Jean was not afraid of mixing brilliant splashes of color into her decor. She possessed an intrinsic sense of fashionable style that allowed her to use multiple colors. Reminded Emma of when she was a little girl, filling in her coloring book, trying to use every color in her crayon box. Emma smiled, somehow Jean made it all work and her home felt not only colorful, but joyful and happy.

Jean brought two steaming hot plates of food to the table. "Okay, here we go, dig in," she said as she sat down.

Emma laughed as she looked at all the food on her plate. "I hope you won't be hurt if I can't eat all this food. I don't care how delicious it is, I would explode if I ate everything you put on this plate."

"I know. Eat what you want, take the rest home. I always make way too much."

Emma took a few bites. "This is really good, one of your better concoctions if I do say so."

"Thanks Em, I like it too. Maybe I'll suggest this dish in one of my columns. Busy working mothers are always interested in good recipes that are fast and easy."

After dinner, Emma helped Jean clean up the kitchen while they chatted.

"Thanks again for the wonderful meal." Emma called out as she walked out of Jean's carrying her leftovers in a Tupperware container. She would have to wait a bit before she exercised tonight but it was totally worth it.

Later that evening, after finishing her workout, Emma was relaxing in her favorite chair, reading a book, when her phone rang. She looked at her watch and noted that it was 9:52 pm. She checked the caller ID. It specified Hartman Inc. Sheesh! A sales call at this hour? I'll fix them, she thought, as she picked up the phone. She dispensed with the polite hello when answering the phone. Instead she demanded; "What do you want? I'm on the National Do Not Call Registry and I want to know how you got this number. In fact, I want your name and the name of your company so I can sue you for calling me after 9 pm."

She waited, but there was no response. Just as she was about to hang up, she heard a man's voice.

"Ah, hello. Is this Emma Mason?" The voice inquired, with noticeable hesitation.

"Who wants to know?" she continued to challenge the caller.

"Emma? This is Peter. Peter Hartman from the Lilac Festival. I'm sorry if I'm calling too late. I wasn't sure what time you got home from work."

"Peter?" Emma felt her face flush and was glad that he couldn't see her. "How? I'm sorry, I don't understand. How did you get this number?"

"Simple really. You told me your last name was Mason, so I just set out to call all the Masons in the phone book until I found someone who knew you. I got lucky because your Uncle Al was the first listing. When I explained that I had met you at the Lilac Festival and wanted to see you again, he was more than happy to help out. He made it clear that he and your Aunt Mona are very fond of you. Said you were their favorite niece. He also said you'd been single too long and that he and your Aunt wanted you to meet a nice guy and settle down."

"He what!" Emma recoiled from the receiver with surprise. She was now embarrassed AND confused. All she could manage to say was, "Oh, he did, did he? And somehow he decided that you were that nice guy?" She paused when she realized she sounded more like a teenager than an adult. She took a deep breath. "I'll have a talk with my Uncle. You could be a dangerous criminal - a stalker - somebody who hates cops! How would he know?"

"Oh, I don't want to give you the wrong impression, he was very careful. He only agreed to give me the address of the building you worked in so I could send you flowers, and this number so I could call. Nothing more. He didn't tell me your home address or I would have sent the flowers there."

"The flowers, oh, sorry, of course, I forgot! Thank you for the flowers and balloons, that was a nice surprise."

"Was it? Then is the answer yes? Will you go out to dinner with me this weekend? I would like to see you again."

"Well, I don't know. I really don't know anything about you."

"I'm sure we can remedy that over dinner, but just so we're on a level playing field, my last name is Hartman. I'm the owner of Peter Hartman Enterprises. My offices are downtown on Fitzhugh Street and I live on Vick Park A, off East Avenue. I do not have a criminal record and I'm a very nice guy. You can ask my mother, or better yet, have dinner with me and you can decide for yourself."

Emma was tempted. It had been months since she had gone out on a date. He certainly sounded like he would be interesting. "All right, but with the condition that I can meet you at the restaurant. I'll also need your cell phone number so I can call you if I have to cancel. I'm a homicide detective, so I don't have regular office hours."

"I understand perfectly. I don't have regular hours either. It's a deal. I'll give you the number of my exchange. They can always get a message to me. I made reservations at Papa Joey's for 7 o'clock Friday evening if that works for you."

"Yes, Friday sounds good."

"Great, I hope you like Italian. It's just a little place on the west side but according to my mother, they have the best sauce in town."

"Sounds great. I've heard good things about Papa Joey's, but I've never been. I'll meet you there at 7 o'clock Friday evening."

"It's a date. I'm looking forward to seeing you again. Sorry for calling after 9, I'll be careful not to do that again. Good-bye for now, Emma."

"Good-bye, Peter and thanks again for the flowers, they're beautiful."

Emma smiled as she hung up the phone. Interesting she thought, he knows I'm a homicide detective and he still wants to see me again. He's resourceful, have to give him that. Also, have to call "Uncle Cupid" and tell him not to ever do that again. He knows that he's supposed to take down the name and phone number of anyone who wants to find me and give ME the information. He knows better. Wonder why he made an exception?

She returned to her book but couldn't concentrate with all the random thoughts bouncing around in her head. Who was Peter Hartman and why was he so determined to see her again?

She thought about past dinner dates and romances that ran out of steam, wondered why they hadn't worked out. Thought about getting a pet that could eat her leftovers. Remembered she had to pay her utility bill this week. Finally, she put the book down and went to bed. Sleep was what she needed, a good night's sleep.

## CHAPTER 9

It had been almost a week since Alexander murdered Max and left him in the alley for the police to find. He had kept abreast of all the media coverage as they reported on the incident. Noting with pleasure the RPD had assigned a female detective to lead the investigation. That fact had only increased his confidence that they'd never be able to connect him to the crime.

He found the detective, Emma Mason, rather fetching but was anticipating her ultimate failure. He also found the media's absence of detail in their reports rather disappointing. Referring to Luther Maxwell only as a "career criminal", without bothering to note his countless crimes against humanity. They failed to mention the numerous people he had robbed. People he had emotionally and physically injured, even murdered just to further his own pitiful existence! The man had been ruthless and barbaric! He was a violent, despicable human being who possessed no remorse. He was no better than a cockroach. The newspaper, in fact this entire city should be celebrating the man's demise, for crying out loud. Alexander was hopeful that the next time the media would be more descriptive when detailing the misspent life of the evil criminal he chose to eliminate for them. He recalled the media coverage of his parents. The continuous dialog about his family's tragedy. Seemed to Alexander that it went on for months, keeping his emotions open and raw like a festering wound that could not heal. The media had become his enemy with their constant coverage of every sordid detail of the murders. Now he felt they had let him down.

Today marked the third day in a row Alexander had sat on these miserable benches. He had positioned himself as an observer in the criminal courtroom so he could listen to the legal proceedings, but that forced him to sit on these hard benches installed for spectators. Alexander shifted his weight often as he tried to find a comfortable position on the hard, unforgiving bench. It was, to his mind, a pathetic substitute for a cushioned bench. He yearned for the soft cushioned pews like the ones he sat on in church… the Catholic church he had attended every Sunday with his mother, bless her soul. Now those were comfortable!

Thinking about his mother relaxed him. He tried to imagine her arms encircling his shoulders again in one of those infrequent hugs he so cherished. Neither mother nor father were particularly demonstrative, and it was rare for her to show him affection as a child, so when she did embrace him, it elevated him to near tears. He longed to reach for the moon just to lay it at her feet. He admired his father, but he worshiped his mother. She was the reason he had envisioned becoming a forensic scientist, solving crimes all over the world. Putting away evil criminals so they could no longer prey on the innocent. His dream was gone now, or was it his mother's dream? She was the one who had rallied against the evil in the world, the crimes against humanity that were never solved. She was the one who raised money to give assistance and aid to the victims of those crimes. The irony of her brutal murder was not lost on him.

The police had caught and charged a man named Jethro Mercier with the murder of his parents. Alexander would never forget the day the case was dismissed and the murderer walked out of court a free man. A technicality the judge had ruled. Alexander had always believed that travesties of that magnitude only happened in Hollywood films. Alexander had never felt such fury. He became obsessed and paranoid. Doctors claimed he lost touch with reality. They whisked him away to that terrible hospital where he was locked up and forced into treatment. As he slowly recovered, his focus returned to his mother. His goal in life had always been to make her proud, and now she was gone. The innocent victim of a horrendous crime herself. A crime that in turn, had made Alexander an innocent casualty as well.

His thoughts wandered to his beloved grandfather and the exclusive men's clothing line that he had designed when he first came to America. His grandfather was a gifted tailor who made customized garments in his home. In due course, he opened one store, then another. Until his family operated factories and retail stores all over the world selling high priced men's wear. 'Wright Wear - Always The Wright Choice for Men of Worth,' was his grandfather's slogan. His ads emphasized the clothing as elegant and distinguished. 'When you have to look your best, it's the Wright choice'. It was the business his grandfather started and his father had devoted his life to building.

His father had branched out into the travel industry because of his extensive experience traveling all over the world in search of outlets. All their hard work had resulted in a life of wealth and privilege for Alexander. Now their fortune was gone. His father's partners had flocked, like vultures, tearing everything apart to get their share. The rest was quickly consumed by the lawyers, doctors and hospital. There was little left to allow Alexander to continue living in the style he was accustomed to. The only thing the lawyers saved was his Lincoln and the family home on East Avenue. Unfortunately, that also included the unpaid bills that came with them. They were the reason he found himself in this position. So desperate for money that he had to devise ingenious ways to raise the income he needed just to live. Finding a "job" was a joke. He wasn't the 9 to 5 type.

Well, that was all behind him now. He had the future to think about. He was determined to somehow regain what he had lost and then perhaps make their name a name to be proud of once again. To do that, he must proceed with his chosen course of action. He was, after all, Alexander Chesterton Wright the Third. The Wright man for the job. He smiled at having just created his own slogan and wondered if his Grandfather would approve.

His thoughts were interrupted by two young people who wanted him to stand so they could move past him on their way out. He wondered if he should leave also, since this trial looked like another dead end. It started out so promising - the defendant, a C.E.O. of his own company, was accused of abusing and then murdering his wife of 21 years. Evidence showed progressive and escalating abuse that ended when he choked her to death. He then attempted to cover it up by claiming he found her body when he returned home from work.

Alexander had listened to all the evidence and felt the prosecutor had presented enough to obtain a conviction. He was sure the jury would see it that way and would find the defendant guilty as charged.

Alexander had come to the courthouse searching for his next project. Killing Max had felt so satisfying that he felt compelled to do it again. All the money he'd confiscated had been an unexpected bonus. Alexander had been able to pay all his bills, but the extra cash would soon run out. He continued to contemplate seeking a real job, but he was first to admit he had no marketable skills. He had never wanted to work for his father in the clothing business, but he did enjoy wearing the exclusive clothing and the best footwear money could buy.

His degree was in criminal justice and the forensic sciences. His career was finished before it started after his unfortunate breakdown and forced residence in the state mental hospital for those five or was it six months? He wasn't sure anymore. Now he found himself totally unprepared to finance the lifestyle that he had become accustomed to.

After his successful experience with Max, he had created guidelines to assist him in the selection process for future 'disposals'. The prospect had to commit at least one murder and gotten away with it. Alexander pictured himself as an advocate for the victims in those cases. When justice was not served, when the truth had been twisted and tangled to the point that it was no longer applicable. He would be the one person dedicated to ensuring that justice would indeed be served. He alone would right the wrong and end the life and crimes of those criminals who fell through the slippery fingers of Lady Justice. The Bible says, "an eye for an eye," so Alexander felt he was doing God's work. But finding these criminals was proving to be more difficult than he had first imagined.

He had thought it was a chance accident, meeting Max when he was leaving the courthouse on that particular day. But perhaps it had not been a simple coincidence. Perhaps that had been God's way of guiding him to his current position as avenger. Now he needed to find a better way to identify his next prospects.

Alexander had thought that silent observation of felony trials was the best option but he now hoped he could find a better way. After sitting on these insufferable benches installed for the hoi polloi for the last three days, he told God He would have to show him another way.

Alexander heard the Judge slam his gavel down as court was called back to order. The activity in the courtroom quieted as the jury filed in. The jury foreman read the verdict: Guilty of first degree murder, as charged. There were sobs and murmurs among the spectators as they quietly filed out of the courtroom discussing the verdict.

He watched as the prisoner, head bowed, was led away in handcuffs. The parents, siblings and children of the convicted man and his murdered wife were divided in their reactions except for the sadness they each displayed.

Alexander was satisfied, but also disappointed. Here was a man who deserved to die for what he had done, but the legal system worked and they got it right this time. Perhaps the courts didn't fail as often as he had thought when he began his research. Didn't matter, the system had let him and his parents down and that was all he cared about. The man who murdered his parents confessed before his lawyer was present, then immediately recanted. None of it could be used in court and without the confession, they didn't have enough evidence left to win a conviction. Ludicrous thought Alexander that the courts allowed that coward to get away with the murder of the only people he had ever loved.

Alexander walked out of the courthouse in deep thought. His mind working hard to think of a better way to find new prospects. His mind whirled with ideas as he struggled to devise the best way to proceed with his research. The psychiatrists had noted that he possessed a high degree of intelligence but also claimed he exhibited signs of antisocial personality disorders. He knew better. He was smarter than them. He just had to apply himself. Perhaps if he went to the library or studied old newspaper stories of cold cases. Too bad he couldn't go right into police headquarters and search their cold case files. He smiled as he pictured himself, walking into police headquarters, showing some kind of special badge with "AVENGER" printed on its shiny surface. He pictured the police giving him the names of people they knew had committed violent crimes, but they lacked the proper evidence to prosecute, or in his case, it was all thrown out of court on a technicality. Those well paid lawyers who were not above manipulating legal resources or loopholes in the laws to get their clients off. It was positively appalling. Even the police would cooperate with him if they could. Yes, he was sure the police would appreciate what he was doing, they just couldn't say so.

He walked out of court, to his car, and drove to his big empty house on East Avenue. The homeowners in this neighborhood, and on this street in particular, were second or third generation wealth. Families with long histories of affluence and prosperity and for the most part, they kept to themselves.

They were nice enough to him after his parents were murdered, more out of curiosity than real concern. Since he had returned from the hospital, there was only one who had remained the least bit neighborly.

The imposing home was built around 1840. All brick, with a large porch that hugged the house, wrapping around the front and sides. The overhanging roof that provided shade for the porch was secured by sturdy columns, embellished at the top with ornate decorations. The hanging baskets of bright, colorful plants that his mother had lovingly placed between the columns each spring were missing. Only the empty hooks remained, waiting with firm resolve, for the baskets of flowers so they could fulfill their destiny. The trimmed shrubs stood as silent sentinels, hiding the weeds that seemed to impart a different look to the home this past year. Other than those subtle changes, you'd never know his parents were gone. Most of the house was obscured from the street by mature trees and bushes that only allowed a glimpse of the colorful rose bushes that decorated the front gardens.

The garage was tucked away in the back, attached to the house by an enclosed breezeway. Alexander's father had built the garage to replace the original carriage house and the breezeway replaced the arbor that had served to connect the original stables and carriage house to the main house.

Alexander drove down the long driveway and parked his car inside the garage. He closed the overhanging door and walked into the breezeway. There was a door at the other end that opened into the main house and two side doors; one leading to the basement and the other to what was once the servants quarters. The servants were gone. They moved out while he was in the hospital. Now that he lived alone, he discovered that he liked the quiet. It was so much easier to hear the faint voices that kept him company and helped him cope.

He had used some of the money he had taken from Max to pay to have his internet service reactivated. Alexander enjoyed sitting down in front of his computer to surf the net. That afternoon he searched the words "cold cases", just for fun. Over 700 cases popped up on his screen, dating back over the last 10 years. Pay dirt, he thought with surprise! Who knew it could be this easy? He said a quick, "thank you", to God as he realized he could stay right here, relaxing at home, in his comfortable chairs, researching these cases at his leisure.

He was surprised by all the detail he could pull off the internet. In particular, he found a site operated by his local newspaper succinctly titled, Cold Case Files. In it he found all the information he would need to find his next target. The problem now was that he had too many options. With God's help, he would find the right words. Words that would enable him to whittle down the possibilities, focus his research to produce a workable number of potential eliminations.

He worked late into the evening searching for the right murderer. He had decided to focus this time on abusive husbands who murdered their wives and somehow were able to walk out of court free men. These last few days of observation in court had allowed Alexander to see, first hand, how destructive domestic abuse was to the entire family, children, parents, grandparents, brothers and sisters - even neighbors were affected. Most of them not knowing what to do or even if they should get involved, then the guilt that comes with hindsight after someone ends up murdered. Everyone wonders, what if I had said or done something? Should I have gotten involved?

After observing the end results all week, Alexander felt he knew the answer to that question. Yes! Say something. Tell someone. Call the police. The more people who know and speak up the less chance the abuser will feel invulnerable. The better the chance one or all of those involved will reach out for help. At the very least, the victims might not feel so isolated and alone.

Alexander had no firsthand knowledge of this unconscionable behavior, his parents were always kind to him and each other. However, he did have a friend in high school, Bobby, who claimed that his father abused him and his mother. Alexander's observations in court had renewed his thoughts about his childhood friend and the unfortunate events that followed.

Alexander knew Bobby's parents personally because he had spent many hours playing at their house. When Bobby confided in him and told him about the abuse, Alexander did not believe him. Bobby's father was a successful businessman and an active member of their church. Alexander would not believe that a man like that could be abusive to his family. Besides, he had observed Bobby's father when he visited their house and thought he was a wonderful parent. He was certain Bobby was just making it up and did not support him.

Years later, he learned that Bobby shot and killed his father after his father had beaten his mother so severely that she almost died. Alexander couldn't help Bobby then. Now he felt guilty for not believing him those many years ago. He felt compelled to make amends by helping another family suffering from the curse of domestic abuse.

Alexander couldn't understand how any man could believe that he could force his wife and children to love him more by using his fists to gain power over them. He felt that these men, these bullies, were the bona fide crazy ones and they needed to be stopped. Those helpless wives and children needed to be protected from this kind of senseless violence. Alexander vowed to do what he could to help them. To prove that somebody cared. He felt he owed it to his friend, Bobby.

## CHAPTER 10

Wednesday morning Emma was working at her desk when Mitch came into her office carrying his coffee and a glazed donut. He was wearing jeans and a sport shirt open at the collar, his gun strapped under his arm. She knew that he would have a nice sport coat to wear that would cover his gun when they were doing interviews, but around the office Mitch was a casual dresser.

She enjoyed having him as her partner. He was a big improvement from her last partner. In fact, Emma had selected Mitch herself and was happy when he accepted. He was an excellent detective. Good looks were just a nice bonus. Emma looked up at him and smiled, "I wish I could eat donuts like you and still keep my figure."

Mitch sat down on the edge of her desk and passed the donut under her nose. "Just blessed with good DNA, that's all."

She slapped at his hand and hit the donut, sending the glaze topping in all directions. Emma knew he was only joking about the DNA. He worked out every morning to keep his body in fighting shape, a habit he'd retained from his Marine training.

"You're in here early, Em. Did we get a break in the case?"

"No, no such luck, I woke up early so I came in to get myself organized. We have two interviews lined up today, I'm hoping we'll get something useful. We still haven't been able to rule out suicide. I ran probabilities on the computer this morning, using the information we've collected so far, and the highest likelihood is divided between Maxwell being murdered by someone he trusted or someone he was attempting to rob. Suicide was only a 14% possibility. We need more information to narrow it down."

Mitch stood up. "I'm thinking we'll get a positive ID from Mr. Lemcke this morning. He should be coming in soon. I'll call you when he gets here."

"Thanks Mitch." She was grateful she had time for another cup of coffee before she would have to talk to anyone else. She glanced at the poster on her wall. It pictured a masked raccoon, standing in Ninja pose, over the caption; LEAVE THE COFFEE POT AND NO ONE GETS HURT.
She could sympathize with the raccoon, she understood how he felt. Coffee was her only addiction.

Twenty minutes later, Mitch called to tell her Mr. Lemcke had arrived and they were waiting for her in interview room C. Emma collected her notes and joined them.

Mr. Lemcke stood when Emma entered the room. He extended his hand to shake hers then waited for her to sit down before he reclaimed his seat.

How nice she thought, old fashioned manners never go out of style. It was refreshing somehow when a man demonstrated good manners in today's world. Mr. Lemcke was tall and slim with the weathered look of a farmer. He was good-natured and comfortable with the detectives.

Mitch took the lead as he introduced himself and Emma. He thanked Mr. Lemcke for coming in. "Our conversation is being recorded. Do we have your permission to continue Mr. Lemcke?"

"Certainly Mitch, but first, please call me Red, everyone does. I do hope I'll be able to help." He was relaxed as he sat back in his chair and smiled at them.

"Thank you, Red. We asked you to come in because we want to talk to you about the robbery that occurred nine years ago when you were shot. We may have a break in the case, and we'd like you to re-examine some of the details of that event for us."

"Sure, I don't know how much detail I remember about it Mitch, but I will be happy to help any way I can. Especially if it helps get that guy off the street. What did you want to know?"

"First of all, for purposes of identification, we need to verify your name and address."

"My given name is Abraham L. Lemcke, I live on Bennett Road in Hilton, New York, on my family's farm."

"Have you lived there all your life?"

"Not yet!" he replied with a chuckle.

Mitch and Emma exchanged amused glances.

"According to our records," Mitch continued, attempting to keep his professional demeanor, "about nine years ago you were robbed and shot in the leg in front of an ATM on Genesee Street. Afterward, you worked with a police sketch artist to develop a composite of the man responsible. We have that sketch and some photos that we would like you to look at to see if you can identify any of them as the man who robbed you. Take your time, we know it's been a while." Mitch handed Red the original composite sketch from nine years ago and then dropped a half dozen photos onto the table for Mr. Lemcke to study. He picked each one up and studied it with care, then put it back down. When he had inspected all of them, he picked up Maxwell's photo and inspected it once again.

"This looks very much like the guy who shot me. I'm not 100 percent sure, it's been a while, but if this was not the man, then he certainly looks a lot like him. Funny, how that face stays in my memory. That instant I heard the gun go off. The smile on his face when I gave in and handed over my money. At first I thought he missed, that it was a warning shot. Wasn't until I felt the blood running down my leg that I realized I'd been shot. He was gone by then. I'd sure like to have a talk with that young man about shooting me like that. I still limp, and the doctors say it will just keep getting worse."

"I'm sorry to say you won't have the opportunity to confront him again. The man you picked out, by the name of Luther Maxwell, has been shot and is currently residing in our morgue."

"Well that's poetic justice for you! I guess it's true, live by the sword, die by the sword, or in his case, the gun."

Emma couldn't help but smile at Mr. Lemcke's response to the news of Maxwell's death. She had to agree, it did seem fitting, still, it was not her job to judge the dead, but to find the facts, the how and why of what had happened.

Mitch gave Mr. Lemcke instructions on how to submit a claim for reimbursement of his original loss caused by the robbery. Then they all stood up and Emma thanked Mr. Lemcke for his assistance. After Red left the room, Emma told Mitch to add the ID to the file, and close the case on Mr. Lemcke's robbery.

"Wish all of our witnesses were that good at giving IDs," Mitch remarked.

"I agree, and I have to say, Mr. Lemcke seems like a very nice man in spite of these circumstances. Reminds me of that old saying, 'bad things do happen to good people'. In his case, he seems to have taken it in stride, hasn't let it destroy his sense of humor. Got to admire a man like that."

Emma walked back to her office to study the transcripts of the trial of Luther Maxwell from three weeks ago. She wanted to know exactly what Reed said when he had alibied Maxwell. At this point, he was the only person with any connection to Maxwell they had been able to identify. Their only POI and they needed to be careful with their interview. She didn't want to overlook anything.

When her stomach began to growl, she was reminded it was time to eat lunch. She walked down the stairs, through the lobby and outside to the street vendors. She looked to her right, then her left, she could see several food carts in each direction, all of them busy serving up their version of fast food. One cart stood out from the others because it had a line waiting to order. The name 'Spot Hots' was emblazoned on the front of the cart. She walked to the end of the line and as she moved forward, she anticipated what she would order.

Jamie and his wife Christy were acknowledging and conversing with each of their customers while Jamie prepared their individual orders. Spot Hots served up the same hot dogs and hamburgers from their cart as the others, but the friendly, personal service was what brought customers back. Everyone was greeted by name. Emma thought one or perhaps both of them must have an impressive memory. Every day they had a special. Today it was pulled pork sandwiches. Emma hoped they wouldn't run out before she could order one.

She quickly moved to the front of the line where Christy greeted her warmly. "Detective Mason, you're looking good, what would you like to order today?"

Emma ordered the pulled pork special with a bag of chips and was delighted to see that Jamie still had an ample supply. "Christy, make that two please, and put them into different bags."

"Sure thing, I'll bet you're taking one back for Mitch, he really likes our pulled pork sandwiches."

"You would win that bet."

Emma returned to her office. She dropped Mitch's sandwich off on his desk. She knew that he would enjoy it, even if he had already eaten lunch. She smiled thinking about it. That man can sure put away the groceries.

# CHAPTER 11

That afternoon, Emma and Mitch drove to Woodlawn Street off Monroe Avenue to talk with Mr. Reed. They parked across the street from his apartment house. The sound of loud music assaulted their ears as soon as they exited their car.

"La musique forte." Mitch muttered.

"Yes, I agree. The neighbors can't be happy about that music, it's way too loud."

As they crossed the street and walked onto the sidewalk, Emma observed a man sitting in a truck parked in a driveway. He was drinking beer with the windows down and the radio blasting country songs.

Emma, badge in hand, walked up to the driver. She flashed her badge, and waited for the moment to register. The man looked at her with bloodshot eyes, then down at her ID. Turning away, she heard him grumble, "Aw, shit!" as he fumbled to turn off the radio. It was a welcome relief when he found his target. He turned back toward her to speak. The stench of stale cigarettes and beer permeated the air as he expelled hissing sounds. It forced Emma to take a step backwards as if she'd been slapped. Mitch was right behind her and stood his ground as Emma backed up and stepped on his foot.

"Oh, ouch!" was all he said as he put his hands on Emma's shoulders in a show of support. She stepped back towards the truck.

At the same moment, the occupant must have decided he would be better off to make a run for it. He opened the door, hitting Emma square in the chest, pushing her backwards again. He jumped out of the truck, landing on his feet, but instead of running away, he crumpled to the ground in a drunken heap. Two empties rolled out with him and went clanging onto the ground. A third bottle, unopened, rolled off the seat and fell with him. As it fell, Mitch reached out and caught it before it landed on Reeds bobbing head.

"Hey! You're stealing my beer! Give that back! Somebody... call the police!" Reed yelled out, having already forgotten that they were the police.

Mitch picked the man up, leaned him against his truck, and asked him if he was Mr. Reed.

A neighbor shouted out that it was Reed and he was happy that the police had finally come to arrest him.

Emma regained her balance and walked over to talk to the neighbors who had swarmed out of their houses to observe. They told her that they had called 911 over an hour ago to complain about the noise and to report that Mr. Reed was drinking in his truck again. When confronted, Reed told his neighbors that as long as he didn't start the engine, he could sit in his truck and drink all day long if he wanted to and they could all just go to hell.

Emma pulled out her cuffs and Mitch held Reed up so she could cuff him. "I'm arresting you for drinking while sitting in the driver's seat of a vehicle with the keys in the ignition. Which, for your information, genius, is against the law in New York State. And just to keep your lawyer busy, I'm going to slap you with a drunk and disorderly, breaking the open container law and littering."

Mitch started to recite the Miranda warning, but Emma stopped him. "Save it Mitch until I get my recorder out. Reed will never remember and we may need to prove that we observed proper procedures." With the recorder on, they repeated the violations, read him his rights and administered the breathalyzer test.

Mitch whistled, then read the BAC results to Emma. "Reed blew a .193. It's no wonder he can't stand up on his own. We'll have to wait a while before we can interview him."

They folded the now complacent Reed into the back seat of the squad car and Emma stood alongside the car to keep an eye on him while Mitch got the camera and went back to document the scene. After collecting the evidence, Mitch pulled the keys out of Reed's truck and locked it. When he was headed back to the squad car, Emma glanced into the back seat, where Reed was now passed out. Oblivious to the world. She helped Mitch put everything into the trunk of the police car. They would turn it all over to evidence when they got back to the station.

As they climbed into their car, the neighbors started cheering and clapping their hands.

Emma smiled at Mitch as they drove away. "Some days it feels good to be a cop."

"Glad we could do something to help this time. Just takes one inconsiderate neighbor to ruin it for everyone in the neighborhood." Mitch eased the car back onto Monroe Avenue. "Did you know that Monroe Avenue was named after President James Monroe?"

"No, but I did know that Monroe Avenue has been described as the spirit and soul of Rochester. I read a magazine article that referred to it as one of the most pedestrian-friendly and hip sections of the city. Lots of unique shops and restaurants that feature outdoor seating. Some even allow customers to keep their dogs with them at the outside tables."

"Amanda loves the art galleries on Monroe. We've ridden our bikes through the area since they added designated bike lanes a few years ago."

"I love that Rochester has made bicycling so accessible over the last few years. In fact, I bought a bike last year to ride on the trails that run along the Erie Canal and Genesee River. I find it very relaxing and the changing seasons make the scenery so diverse."

"I'm not much of a bicyclist, I prefer my bikes with a throttle. But I'll ride with Amanda now and then because she loves it so much. I do like the four seasons we enjoy here in Rochester. I mean they're each so distinctive and well-defined. Winter is snowmobile season, spring is Jeep season, summer is boating and jet ski season, and fall is quad season. It's a nice balance, keeps life interesting. I can't choose one season over the other. That's why I live here, so I don't have to."

"Sheesh, it doesn't take a detective to see the pattern in your interests, they're all motorized!"

"Don't sell me short, I have a lot of interests, I think of myself as a modern day Renaissance man. Proficient in a wide variety of fields. In fact, I just signed up with the Finger Lakes Soaring Club to learn how to operate a glider down in Dansville. No motor, in fact, it's called motorless flight."

"Sorry, I stand corrected" Emma said as they pulled into the receiving area of the jail, where they unloaded their unconscious passenger.

## CHAPTER 12

Thursday morning Alexander awoke refreshed and anxious to resume his research. He had identified his next target, the nefarious, Edward O. Jackson.

This morning he planned to compile all the details he could uncover regarding Jackson's life and crime. A man who had made a name for himself as a professional tennis player. To the public it looked like he had it all; beautiful wife, healthy children, fame, and all the money that came with it. But behind the scenes, police reports documented the numerous times they had been called to the Jackson home for domestic disturbances. Long before the actual murder. His wife's hospital records showed a history of injuries resulting from his cruel and abusive behavior over the seven years they were married until she finally found the strength to stand up to him and started divorce proceedings.

Alexander's research into domestic violence cases had often mentioned that this was the most dangerous period of time for the victim. The abuser realizes he's no longer in control and will stop at nothing until he has regained dominance. It proved true in this case, as the relationship ended for good when Jackson murdered his wife in the basement of their California home. He watched as she bled to death from the numerous stab wounds he had inflicted, while their three children slept.

Two years later, he was tried for her murder, but his expensive team of lawyers managed to let him dance away in spite of all the evidence against him. At least he lost custody of his children as the result of a civil suit brought by relatives of his wife.

Edward O. Jackson relocated after he lost custody of his children and now lived in relative anonymity in Alexander's own neighborhood. He was even a member of the same Oakview Country Club. Mr. Jackson had a Facebook page and a blog that offered more than enough detail about his current likes and dislikes, his hobbies, favorite restaurants, bars, and even the names of his current friends.

Alexander submerged himself in all the details he could dredge up regarding Jackson's life. Before and after the murder.

As he collected his information, he formed a tentative plan for the disposal of someone he regarded as a piece of human waste. Jackson used a knife, so therefore, Alexander thought it only fitting to eliminate him with one. He was motivated by the many Bible passages that sanctioned taking a life. He felt he was following God's own instructions when he read Deuteronomy 19:20-21. "You shall purge the evil, show no pity: life for life, eye for eye."

As Alexander went about his business that day, he sang to himself. Songs he had learned in church. He felt light hearted and content now that his life had meaningful direction. He was examining areas of his home looking for a suitable location to carry out this new task. The fruit cellar in the basement was a good possibility, since there was a drain in the floor. He surmised he would need it to be able to dispose of all the blood - no need to make more work for himself.

He climbed the stairs back to the first floor and looked down the hallway towards the garage. His gaze fell on the door to the servants' quarters. Another possibility. The rooms had been empty for months. He moved toward the door, unlocked it, and walked into the small kitchen.

Looking around the room, he spotted the door leading to the large bathroom just off the kitchen. He smiled when he remembered the extra-large old fashioned claw foot tub in the center. Walking into the bathroom, he realized this would be even better, a new plan formulated in his mind. The room was close to the garage, there were no stairs to climb and the tub was the perfect size. The tubs location worked as well, he would have room to move around it. Yes, this would be most suitable.

Next he needed to purchase supplies, and he would have to buy them in a way that could not be traced back to him. He decided that a quick trip to neighboring Toronto, Canada, with cash, was the safest way to obtain everything he would need. He gathered his passport and packed the few things he might need before he climbed into his car and drove away.

Depending on the traffic, it would be a three to four hour drive. Alexander had made this drive often as a child with his parents, now he was going by himself. There were several enjoyable routes to choose from on this sunny Spring day. Alexander chose the route that ran along the picturesque Lake Ontario Parkway. The route was referred to as the Seaway Trail and was part of the National Scenic Byway that ran from Pennsylvania to Lake Erie. This section meandered back and forth between the shoreline, the plowed fields and the numerous orchards that dotted western New York State.

Enjoying the scenery brought to mind his experiences when he traveled outside the state. How people reacted when he said he lived in New York. They imagined cement and tall buildings because they pictured New York City. They had no idea how really rural the majority of the state was. Why one young man from Texas had once asked him if he had ever seen a live cow! He told him that yes, of course he had, then added that we have zoos in Western New York. He chuckled again as he passed a large herd of milk cows in the nearby pasture.

Alexander used this time to continue examining and refining his plan. Over and over he contemplated probabilities, examined every possible contingency. He continued honing the plan until he was satisfied that he would be committing another perfect crime. They'd never catch him, he assured himself. The very thought made him feel proud, but the feeling was followed by deep disappointment that all his altruistic efforts would go unrecognized. No one would ever know of his accomplishments, his diligence and dedication to public service. His unselfish devotion to assure that justice would ultimately be victorious. Well, he thought, anonymity was the price he had to pay in order to continue his mission to bring justice to victims consigned to oblivion by our flawed court system. He'd revel alone at his self-sacrificing actions that he had undertaken in order to make the world a better place for everyone.

Perhaps he should compose a journal so that after his death, the world could know of his extraordinary deeds. He would dedicate the journal to his childhood friend Bobby, to acknowledge all his friend had endured. In fact, that detective, Emma Mason, the one assigned to the case would no doubt find it interesting to read as well. She would understand then why she never had a chance of capturing him. She would admire his unerring pursuit of justice. She would want to bestow him with honors, posthumously of course. In his imagination there was no limit to Emma's gratitude and admiration.

During his time on the computer, Alexander had taken time to research Emma's career and was pleased to learn that she was a capable and honorable officer. He liked the adage, "Keep your friends close and your enemies closer". Who said that? He couldn't remember. Rommel? Julius Caesar? Maybe it was Michael Corleone in The Godfather? Meh - doesn't matter who said it, only that it's a great strategy. Alexander considered Emma a friend, and he pictured them as a crime-fighting team.

He fulfilled the role of the mighty hunter, avenging injustices unencumbered by rules and laws, and she was the professional guide, cleaning up after him, and putting everything in its proper place in the world. He could almost hear her gentle voice, informing those unfortunate victims that the perpetrator was dead. No longer able to hurt anyone again. He blushed from the pure satisfaction of it.

The drive to Toronto flew by with Alexander deep in thought and perfectly content. He could not remember a time when he had been so pleased with the direction of his life. He had always enjoyed visiting Toronto, it was an exciting and vibrant city. He decided to turn the trip into a mini-vacation to celebrate his genius. His budget only allowed for a room at a mid-range hotel on Yonge Street but he eased his distress with the knowledge that he would soon have more money to spend courtesy of Mr. Jackson.

It was still early afternoon by the time he finished shopping and loading everything into the trunk of his car. Alexander decided it would be a good time to visit the Toronto Public Library on Yonge Street. They had an extensive collection of works by Sir Arthur Conan Doyle and were now featuring an exhibit entitled Adventures with Sherlock Holmes.

He read that they had upwards of 12,000 items in their collection and it sounded like a great way to pass the time, enjoying an afternoon in the company of the great detective. Perhaps when he wrote his journal he would fashion it after Watson's method of short stories. One for each of his adventures in murder. Ah, there, I have even found my title, he thought, completely satisfied with the way everything seemed to be falling into place.

When evening came and the clock in the library indicated it was after 5, Alexander decided he needed to find a place to assuage his hunger. He exited the library and strolled down Yonge Street, away from his hotel, until he found a quaint sidewalk cafe where he could sit outside and watch all the busy people scurrying by. After placing his order, he occupied his time by looking at their faces, wondering how many of them deserved to live and how many deserved to die. He continued thinking about the strangers walking past his table, while he enjoyed his meal.

When his dinner was complete, he was reluctant to leave so he ordered an after dinner drink. Sipping his digestif of Grand Marnier, he continued to imagine intricate scenarios for taking the lives of the people around him. So near, yet they were oblivious to him sitting there as they innocently went about their business. Some passed so close to his table that he could reach out and touch them. He longed for the ability to read minds, to hear the silent thoughts of guilty consciences as they passed by. Unknowingly revealing their darkest secrets to him. He would be able to tap into the repetitive loop of shame and remorse running through their heads. It would be an excellent way to find targets and to relieve them of their pain filled existence. It was a win-win in his opinion. He'd be doing them all a favor. But then he realized, with a sick feeling, that evil people have no remorse. They are cunning and skillful at explaining away their actions. Making themselves seem righteous, even in the sight of God. They would compartmentalize whatever troubled them and move on. It wouldn't do to read their minds. These evil people justified their thoughts to themselves and then believed their own lies. Yes, he knew he was on the right track, disposing of them was the only way. Finishing his last swallow of Grand Marnier, he stood and dropped cash on the table as he looked around with disdain at all the liars. Well, he thought, at least I'm honest with myself. What more could a person hope for?

He moved out to the sidewalk and began walking at a steady pace, blending in with the passersby. He looked forward to the long walk back to his hotel room after his large meal and was glad to get a little exercise. I'm going to turn in early, he thought. I need to be at my best, I owe it to this world I live in. He was elated with his new understanding of how truly twisted and misguided people were. He felt ecstatic and happy with his revelation.

"Marvelous" he said aloud as he visualized his life as a glowing beacon of truth and justice. His life was back on track. "Life is positively marvelous".

# CHAPTER 13

Emma asked Mitch to check the drunk tank to see how Mr. Reed had fared overnight. She hoped that Reed had sobered up enough so they could interview him.

It was late morning before the three of them were set up in the interview room. Reed had not asked for a lawyer so they could talk to him without waiting for his attorney. Emma noted Reed's flushed face, shaking hands and slurred speech. The stench of alcohol still surrounded him like a swarm of bees circling the hive. Hard core alcoholic, she wrote in her interview notes. She motioned to Mitch to take the lead.

Mitch identified Emma and himself first, then informed Reed that cameras were recording the interview. He asked Reed to verify that he had waived his rights to a lawyer and had agreed to talk with them regarding his testimony in the Luther Maxwell Trial.

Reed lifted his head to look at Mitch then Emma. He shrugged his shoulders and mumbled. "Whatever."

"Just to refresh your memory, Mr. Reed. Your testimony provided Mr. Luther Maxwell with an alibi for that day in March - the day of a break in and robbery that he was charged with. You testified in court four weeks ago, that you and Luther Maxwell were drinking together in your truck for the entire day. Is that correct?"

"I think so, yes, we were drinking in my truck that day."

"And do you remember what day that was?"

"Nooo… " he drew the word out, taking time to arrange his thoughts before he continued. "I don't remember exactly, but Luther did! He told me what day to tell the Judge. Ya can ask him when it was. Yeah, ask Luther. I can't keep track no more, ya see. One day's the same as another since my wife left me, and for no good reason I'm tellin' ya. I was good to her, ya see, don't ya?"

"So Luther told you what day he was with you?"

"That's what I said isn't it? See Luther's a smart one. You ask him, see for yourself, he'll tell ya. Could I have something to drink here? I'll be a lot more help to ya if I have a drink, do ya know where I left my truck?" Reed stood up and started patting his pockets, becoming more agitated as he realized they were empty.

"Hey, somebody stole my keys, and my smokes too! What kind a… "

Mitch interrupted Reed's rambling, "Mr. Reed. Please, sit back down. Can you try to focus?"

"I am focused, ya need to ask Luther, like I said. Now can I go?" He moaned as he sat back down, burying his head onto his folded arms on top of the table.

"Not yet, Mr. Reed, I'm sorry to inform you that we can't ask your friend Luther, His body was found in an alley a week ago. Do you know anything about that?"

Reed snapped his head up. Disbelief came over his face as he digested this information.

"Body? You meant like in dead body? No, you have the wrong man, we were drinking together just a few days ago. He bought me a case of beer to thank me for helping him in court last week." Reed's face reflected the effort he was exerting trying to gather his thoughts. To make sense of what Mitch was telling him.

"You helped him out over three weeks ago, he's been dead for a week."

"That's impossible, ya got it wrong, can't be Luther I'm tellin' ya, we were just together. How could this happen? Are ya sure it was Luther?" Reed's confusion was apparent as he stood again, then collapsed into the chair.

"Yes, we're sure Mr. Reed. We're sorry for your loss."

Reed bowed his head and began whimpering.

Emma signaled Mitch to step into the hall so she could talk to him in private. "His brain cells are still soaked in alcohol; time is meaningless to him." she said.

"Agreed. There's no way that Reed killed Maxwell. It's obvious he was unaware of his death plus I doubt he's capable of planning and executing anything more complex than obtaining his next drink."

"Add perjury to his list of charges and get him arraigned as soon as possible. Tell the DA I recommend pleading him out on all charges if he agrees to inpatient rehab and a long probation period. Let's see if we can get him some help to straighten his life out."

"It's worth a shot, but I doubt it will work, he's pretty far gone." Mitch shook his head.

"As long as there's life, there's hope. Let me know if there's anything solid we can do to get him into a program. At least it will give his neighbors relief for a few months if nothing else."

"Got it, but that puts us back to square one on Maxwell's death. What's next?"

"Not sure Mitch. I'm going back over everything to see if there is something we missed while you take care of Reed. If this was murder, and I still think it was, then it could be one we'll never solve."

"I hate it when we have to turn one of our cases over to cold case." Mitch shook his head again. He paused before entering the interview room, "Say, after I finish with Reed, do you want to grab some lunch? The sun's shining and the hot dog carts are lining up as we speak. We could even eat outside if it's not raining yet."

"Sounds good to me. Call me when you're ready. I'll be in my office catching up on paperwork."

"I'll pick you up on my way out."

"Works for me, oh, by the way, great work on the Sullivan disappearance. I just heard this morning that you are being honored for your breakthrough and recovery of Timmy in that case. Way to think outside the box."

Mitch blushed, "I was just glad that we found him alive. We worked close with Missing and Exploited Children on that case. Now that's a great organization." Mitch paused, "I appreciate your comments Em, but I did have a lot of help from them, the FBI team and our own officers. Everyone worked together to recover Timmy. It was a joy when we were able to reunite him with his parents."

Mitch was still smiling when he entered the interview room to deal with the bewildered and distressed Mr. Reed.

## CHAPTER 14

Friday morning Emma was sitting at her desk attempting to address the stack of paperwork that had accumulated overnight. Her thought process seemed to have a mind of its own and she would find herself instead, thinking about her upcoming date that evening with Peter Hartman. Her concentration continued to drift while she contemplated whether her case of nerves was because it had been so long since she last dated, or because she found Peter to be so different then the men she had dated. She did think he was good looking in the comfortable style of the boy next door. She liked the way he projected confidence and radiated energy. She even liked his voice, so clear and pleasant to listen to. She didn't want to admit, even to herself, how much she was looking forward to their upcoming date. She wondered if he was thinking about her as well.

She and Jean had already picked out what clothes she'd wear, including borrowing Jean's fancy open toed shoes. Emma knew she was going to have to spend some money shopping after an honest appraisal of her closet revealed she did not own one decent pair of dressy shoes. The lining on the pair she had always relied on had disintegrated in the three or so years since she last wore them and she'd been forced to throw them away.

They had enjoyed cleaning out her closet last night as they plowed through her sparse wardrobe. That is until Jean discovered the floor length, flannel nightgown hanging in the back of her closet. Emma had forgotten about it. A gift from her mother when she moved out to live on her own. Jean couldn't contain her laughter as she held it up to herself and started to sway around the room while she sang, '*I'm in the mood for love, simply because you're near me.*' "Did this come with a flannel night cap as well?" Jean had asked, with tears rolling down her cheeks.

Emma chuckled out loud remembering how hard they had laughed last night.

Her thoughts were interrupted when Mitch threw open the door to her office and announced they had a break in the Maxwell case. "We've recovered Maxwell's gun!"

"Really! Where? How?" Emma's attention was back on the job.

"Turns out, it was one of those lucky breaks we get every once in awhile. Two patrolmen were working traffic yesterday when they stopped two teenage boys for speeding. They spotted a bag of marijuana in the back seat so they arrested the boys and impounded the car. When the teens were questioned, with their lawyer, they asked for a plea deal. Their lawyer said they had important evidence regarding a body they found in an alley. Turns out they were the boys who first found Maxwell's body. They admitted taking the gun. Police recovered and tested it yesterday. I just got the report this morning from ballistics. It was the missing gun that killed Maxwell. The boys are still here with their lawyer, so we can talk to them this morning before they are released to their parents."

"That's great news! Let's talk with those young men. Set it up as soon as possible."

When Emma and Mitch walked into the interview room, Emma observed that the boys appeared to be unsettled after being processed through booking and spending the night in jail. Emma knew when the officers had newbies under their care, they would NOT go out of their way to make them comfortable. In fact, just the opposite, most police believed in the procedure of shocking them straight, hoping that once through the system would be enough. The smart ones would choose not to place themselves in that position a second time. These boys looked like they had gotten the message loud and clear after being subjected to the official, but unpleasant steps that led up to this point. She just hoped their parents would follow through. Their lawyer was present and introduced the boys to the detectives.

"This is Wayne Holden and Tyrone Williams, they have agreed to answer questions regarding the gun they found, nothing more.

Are we all agreed?"

Emma agreed, then introduced herself and Mitch before proceeding. She confirmed that the boys had been read their rights, and that their lawyer was present.

"Now Wayne, please tell us, in your own words how you boys came into possession of that gun."

"It was Friday afternoon, a week ago, and we were skipping school when we saw the truant officer driving toward us. We quick like, ducked into this alley. That's when we saw this man just layin' there. We would've run back out but we didn't want to get caught, so we hid. When the coast was clear, we checked on the man, but he was dead. He was holding this gun so we took it with us, that's all we took, right Tyrone?"

"Yeah, that's just the way it was."

"You didn't take his money?"

"No," they both answered.

"We can't help you if you don't tell us the truth. Your footprints indicated that you moved and searched the body."

The boys looked at each other, Tyrone shrugged his shoulders,

"Truth is, we did look to see if he had money, but we didn't find none."

"He's telling the truth ma am; we didn't find no money." Wayne agreed.

"Exactly where was the gun when you discovered the body Tyrone?"

"In his hand."

"Where was the hand that was holding the gun?"

"It was sitting on his chest like this," he placed his right hand across his chest. "There was a garbage bag on top of it. I saw the gun when I moved the bag to see if he was dead or alive."

"You're sure about that? The gun was in his hand, his hand was resting on his chest and there was a garbage bag on top of it?"

"Yeah, that's how it was. We didn't take anything else, just the gun, and we put the bags back over him again. We took the gun home and hid it in Wayne's garage and that's where it stayed until yesterday."

"All right boys, you can go home now. I'm not charging you with interfering with a police investigation, at this time. As long as you both go back to attending school. I hear about you skipping again and I'll rethink my decision.

Counsellor, please make sure your clients and their parents understand the seriousness of these charges and the possible consequences of their actions."

Wayne spoke up. "Wait, you promised we'd get a deal."

"You did get a deal," Emma leaned over the table so she could look him in the eye. "We dismissed the speeding and possession charges. We never discussed your interfering with a police investigation by removing and concealing pertinent evidence. That is a serious crime that could result in imprisonment, fines, or both." She stood back up. "Counsellor, please make sure everyone understands my position and these boys are back in school tomorrow." She looked at the two boys again. "Trust me, school is much safer than jail for boys your age. Besides that, once you've completed high school, it's much easier to get a job with school on your resume' instead of prison. So take advantage of this one chance I'm offering you and don't blow it."

Emma and Mitch left the interview room to let the lawyer deal with his clients. They walked up the stairs to Jack's office. As usual, Jack was busy working on papers scattered in what seemed to be a haphazard manner about his desk. It appeared out of control, but Emma knew that Jack had the ability to find structure in the chaos. They waited until Jack finished what he was doing and looked up at them.

Emma summarized the new information for Jack to add to his report, then asked. "Considering their claim that they found the gun on Maxwell's chest, under a bag of garbage, what conclusions can you draw as to what may have happened?"

"Well, we know from the evidence that Maxwell was standing when he was shot through the heart, he died instantly, then his body slid down the wall to the ground. The bag could have fallen on him after he hit the ground, but gravity should have caused the hand with the gun to fall away from the body after it went off. Let me research that and I will get back to you, but my guess right now is that the scene was staged after he was shot, to make it appear that he shot himself. Now all you two have to do is figure out who shot Maxwell and why. I'll put my guys on it, have a report for you by Monday, but I think at this point, we can rule out suicide."

Emma and Mitch returned to the stairs, "Well, I guess that makes it official, we have a murder victim and no leads."

"So what now?" asked Mitch as they walked down the stairs.

"Just going back to my paperwork, we don't have any leads left to run down. Gives both of us time to get caught up and maybe one of us will think of a new angle. We'll decide Monday after we get Jack's report, whether to turn this one over to cold case. Have a good week-end Mitch."

"You too. Enjoy your date but keep your guard up. Later Em." Mitch turned and walked back to his office.

"Always do," she answered as she turned and walked in the opposite direction, headed towards her office.

Emma spent the rest of the day trying to concentrate on her paperwork, while thoughts of Peter and their upcoming date danced uninvited through her head. She often directed her gaze toward the clock on her wall. It seemed to Emma that it might be enchanted as the hands appeared to be moving slower and slower as the afternoon wore on.

## CHAPTER 15

"Jean, stop fussing! You'd think I'd never had a date in my entire life," Emma exclaimed in mock frustration, even as she checked herself in her floor length mirror for the fifth time. "Truth be told, I am a bit nervous, I don't know why."

"Well, you look beautiful in that dress, and you can't see the gun you're wearing under it at all. Why are you wearing it anyway?"

"I've been a cop for so long, I don't feel dressed unless I have it on me. It's second nature to me now. I think about how to conceal my gun with every clothing purchase I make. Like the people with tattoos who buy clothes that show off their body art."

"I guess that makes sense, I always get a pedicure when I can wear sandals and everyone can see my toes. Let's talk about your date, are you excited?"

"I am! Peter has sent me a card every day since I met him. They are always funny and make me laugh. He seems respectful and hasn't pushed to find out where I live or bothered me in any way. In fact, other than the cards, he hasn't contacted me since Tuesday. The card that came today said he was looking forward to seeing me tonight. The picture on the front showed an excited puppy jumping into the air. Inside it said, 'When I think about you my spirits soar!' Isn't that cute?"

Jean thought about it for a minute, "It's either cute or creepy, I don't know which way I want to feel about this guy. Do you know anything about how he treats his mother? There are studies that claim there is a strong connection to the way a man treats his mother and his sisters, that accurately predicts how he will treat his future wife or girlfriend."

"No, sorry to say, I don't have any idea about that. Not yet anyway. Wait, now that I think about it, he did mention his mother several times during our phone conversation."

"What did he say about her?"

"Just that his mother liked this particular restaurant and she would verify that he was a nice guy."

"Well that tells us something. At least he respects her opinion. I just think some of his activities are close to the actions of men who hate women. They prey on smart, confident women like yourself. Part of their M.O. is fooling women into thinking they have good intentions by giving them excessive quantities of flowers, candy, cards and gifts at the start of the relationship. Then they change into monsters." Jean raised her hands into claws and pretended to attack Emma.

Emma stepped back, out of her reach. "Whoa, calm down girlfriend! Watch out for my hair! I know what you mean about men who hate women. My cop sense tells me to be careful, there is something about the guy that's off, but the woman in me still hopes to find a nice guy to spend time with once in awhile. At least I know that being a cop has not destroyed the dreamy romantic in me. Oh well, I'll know more about him after tonight. How do I look?"

"I proclaim you look unforgettably amazing! Have fun and be safe. I have a date tonight myself so off we go."

"OMG Jean, I feel sorry for your date, you're in a rambunctious mood if ever I saw one."

It was a twenty-minute drive to the restaurant. Enough time for Emma to have second thoughts about her decision. She thought over what she knew about the man and had to admit, she didn't know much. I should have run a quick background check on him like Mitch suggested. She felt safe enough driving herself and meeting him at the restaurant, that gave her some advantage. She could leave any time she felt uncomfortable. Without thinking, she reached for her holster and found comfort in the knowledge that her gun was there if she needed it. Her next thought was that she was being silly. Jean's comments must have triggered her anxieties and she was blowing everything out of proportion. Just nerves, she decided. It's been too long since she had been able to relax and spend quality time with someone of the opposite sex. She decided she was going to relax and enjoy herself. She saw the restaurant coming up on her left, put on her turn signal and pulled into the parking lot.

Emma saw Peter standing in front of the entrance to the restaurant. She waved to acknowledge him, then parked her car. She walked across the parking lot while he kept a protective eye on her. He greeted her with a friendly hug, then held the restaurant door for her to enter.

Papa Joey's was a small restaurant with a waiting area and two small dining areas with tables.

The hostess nodded her head when they entered, "Welcome Mr. Hartman, right this way."

They followed her past the first dining room full of customers, into a smaller room that was empty. She led them to a table in front of a warm crackling fire.

Peter held the chair for Emma as she sat down. "I hope you enjoy red wine with your dinner, I selected a light blush that compliments Italian cuisine. If you don't like it, I'll order something else."

Peter sat down across from Emma. A waiter appeared from the shadows, carrying a bucket of ice that cradled a chilled bottle of wine. The waiter uncorked the wine with great ceremony and presented it to Peter who performed his ceremonial duties with experienced ease. Peter give his approval as Emma watched the presentation with fascination. The waiter poured their drinks and returned the bottle to the ice bucket, taking care to thrust the bottle deep into the ice. He placed the bucket on a stand alongside their table then departed into the shadows.

Emma lifted her glass and Peter offered a toast, "Here's hoping we have an enchanted evening, and thank you Emma, for taking a chance and agreeing to have dinner with me tonight."

Emma clinked glasses with Peter and they tasted the wine together.

"The wine is elegant, your toast was delightful and I am sure dinner will be delicious."

Peter nodded his head to acknowledge her comment, then bending forward he whispered, "you look truly amazing Emma, I swear, you are even prettier than I remembered."

Emma blushed, embarrassed by this unaccustomed flattery.

Peter picked up a small box that had been sitting on the table next to his napkin. "I bought something for you the other day, I hope it's not presumptuous of me to buy you a gift since this is our first date, but when I saw it in the window, I wanted you to have it. He handed her the box wrapped with silver paper and topped with a big purple bow.

"I don't know what to say."

"Please, open it before you say anything."

Emma unwrapped the paper and opened the box. Inside was a beautiful gold St. Michael Medal on a thick gold chain. She picked it up and read the words on the front, "Patron Saint of

Law Enforcement Officers." The back was custom engraved, "May he protect you as you protect others."

"Peter, it's beautiful, but I can't accept this."

"I had it engraved, so I can't return it." Peter rose from his chair and walked behind her. He lifted the necklace from her hand and placed it around her neck. She felt his hand on her neck, as he gently moved her hair out of the way so he could secure the chain. She lifted her hand and fingered the medal.

Peter squeezed her shoulders. "Please wear it always for protection."

Emma sighed. She didn't know what she had expected, but this was not it. She had never felt so sheltered and exposed at the same time. She was being swept off her feet and wasn't sure if she should fight the current or relax and enjoy the ride. Under most circumstances, her instincts kicked in and she knew what to do, but everything was off balance tonight, like the world had somehow spun out of control then slipped off its axis and abandoned her to fend for herself.

"Peter, it's beautiful and thoughtful, but you really shouldn't."

"Just say you will wear it always, no strings attached. You deserve it for all your hard work protecting and serving the public for the last fifteen years."

"Well, thank you then." Emma chose to ignore the little red flags that sprang up. She didn't want to ruin the evening by being a suspicious cop. Tonight she was just a lady on a date with a very fascinating gentleman, who knew how long she had been a cop...

The waiter appeared with an assortment of very small steaming plates of food, each one looking more scrumptious than the next. He set them on the table with a flourish then disappeared again.

"You said you had never been to Papa Joey's before so I wasn't sure what to recommend. I asked them to create this little assortment. Each plate contains a sample of their house specialties. Everything is delicious at Papa Joey's, so taste the samples and then we can make our selections. This way I know you will enjoy whatever you decide to order."

"Well, thank you again, that is very considerate, but isn't it also very expensive?"

"What good is having money Emma, if you can't enjoy the benefits every now and again."

"I can't find fault with your rationalization so I will just try this one first." Emma picked up the plate of greens and beans and slid a sample onto her plate.

They continued exchanging small talk while enjoying the delicious bites of food between sips of wine. When they had narrowed down their dinner choices, Peter signaled the waiter who appeared so quickly that Emma was sure he must have been watching them.

"Ready to order Mr. Hartman?"

Emma noted that the waiter did not have an order pad but simply acknowledged each order by repeating it and nodding.

Peter provided their order based on Emma's preferences, and the waiter responded with a brief "Sir" before leaving their table.

He returned minutes later with their salads and a basket full of warm bread. As they relaxed and nibbled on their first course, Emma commented on the fact that they were still alone in the dining room. There were several other tables set up, but they remained empty.

"I prearranged with the owner to have this room to ourselves. I prefer not to be crowded when I dine. I do hope you enjoy the privacy as much as I do."

Emma again found herself at a loss for words. Peter existed in a world that was so different than hers. She wondered for a minute what could make him come on so strong. She wondered if he dated often, and whether he went overboard with all of his dates or if he was just pouring it on for her benefit. Again, she chose to suppress her misgivings and enjoy the evening for what it was. A dinner date. C'mon, Emma she told herself. The guy is smitten. Just go with it. Everything doesn't have to be a mystery that needs to be solved. She fought with herself to stay loose, be fluid, go with the flow.

Peter seemed to note her trepidation and as if reading her mind, reached across the table to take her hand in his. "Emma, I find you to be one of the most fascinating women that I have ever met. You are not only beautiful but you are intelligent, and make your living outwitting murderers and solving crimes. You deal with the abhorrent evil that is rampant in our world and yet you exhibit great charm temperament and grace. I admire you, and I hope that we will be able to spend the days, and perhaps the months ahead, getting to know each other better."

Emma was touched, she placed her free hand over his and squeezed it. "I think I would like that too, Peter."

The rest of the dinner was relaxing and engaging. They spoke without effort while exchanging thoughts and ideas about many subjects including how good Peter's business was doing, her job and how her current cases were coming along. He seemed interested in the day to day routine that was police work.

When dinner was completed and dishes cleared, they ordered coffee. Then reluctant to end the evening, they ordered after dinner drinks. It was Emma who began the exit dance. "Peter, that was a wonderful meal. I'm at a loss to find the words to tell you how much I enjoyed this evening. You are amazing and I'm so pleased that we had this chance to get to know each other better. Thank you so much." She sat back in her chair.

"Please Emma, I'm the one who should thank you. I can't remember the last time I enjoyed myself this much. The evening flew by."

Emma smiled as she stood up.

Peter stood and tossed some money on the table, nodded to the waiter as he moved to Emma's side. He put his arm around her waist, "Allow me to walk you to your car."

They walked out of the empty restaurant to a chorus of goodbyes from the staff.

"My God, Peter, what time is it?

"It's after 11."

"Are we the last ones to leave? How embarrassing, the staff must have been waiting for us to leave so they could go home."

"We are the last to leave, but don't worry about the staff, they were well compensated for making our evening so memorable."

Peter held Emma's hand as they walked to her car. "I hope the next time you will allow me to drive so the evening can last a bit longer."

When they arrived at Emma's car, he took hold of her shoulders and held her so they faced each other.

Emma spoke first. "Thank you again for a beautiful evening Peter."

Peter's face drew closer as he lifted her chin and gently rubbed his lips across hers in a move that sent hot shivers of desire down her spine. "I hate to say goodbye without knowing when I'll see you again Emma. How about Sunday? If you aren't busy for lunch, would you like to visit my home? We could have a picnic on my patio. Would you think about it?"

"Yes, I would like that. You can call me tomorrow to give me your address."

"My address is printed here, on my personal card," he pulled a card out of his pocket and folded it into her hand, then gently lifted her hand and kissed it.

"Goodbye for now Peter, thank you again for an unforgettable evening. The necklace is lovely, but I do hope you aren't going to make a habit of giving me gifts every time we meet."

"I make no promises. Be safe Emma, I'm already looking forward to Sunday." He leaned in again, this time for a warm hug that she returned.

Emma drove home with a smile on her lips and a song in her heart. She was looking forward to tomorrow so she could tell Jean all about it. She had no idea where this was going, but she planned to enjoy it, however temporary it was bound to be.

## CHAPTER 16

Early the next morning, Emma heard a loud thumping sound but had incorporated it into her dream. When she finally opened her eyes, the drama that had been streaming through her brain disappeared. She struggled to understand where the noise was coming from when she heard it again. As the fog cleared, she realized, it's Jean!! Knocking at my door! A quick glance at the clock told her it was after Nine. She struggled to untangle herself from the blankets so she could sit up. She jumped out of bed, grabbed her robe and hurried to open the door.

"Who's there?"

"Are you alone?" Jean whispered.

"Oh for heaven's sake Jean! And what would you say if I said no?"

"You'd see the disappearing act I perfected as a child."

"Well, save the act for another time. I came home alone."

Emma unlocked and opened the door to let Jean in.

"So spill, girlfriend. How did it go? What happened? Are you going to see him again? Hey, wait just a minute, what's that hanging around your neck?"

"Oh, it's a necklace Peter gave me, and to answer your questions, it went great, lots, and yes."

"Never mind that! Let me see that necklace. Holy moly, it's beautiful Em. Now it's getting interesting. Do you have anything I can use for my next column?"

"No, well yes. oh, I don't know. Let me use the bathroom, brush my teeth, get myself together then I'll tell you all about it and you can tell me what you think. Why don't you put on a pot of coffee while you wait? You know where everything is."

Soon the two friends were sitting in the kitchen going over the details of the big Friday night date. Jean made all the appropriate sounds as she listened, spellbound by each event Emma shared with her.

"Emma, can you imagine having so much money that you can just rent an entire room at a restaurant like that? How can I turn that into a column?"

"How about a column on how to really, really, really, impress a woman?"

"Yea, but you left out the part that they also have to be really, really, really, rich."

"I guess that would be a problem for the average guy. Well, believe it or not, I'm still full from dinner last night so I am going to skip our usual Saturday morning breakfast and use all this excess energy to clean my condo this morning. How about I pick you up at noon for our workout at the Y?"

"Sounds good, I have laundry I can do, see you at noon."

That afternoon, Jean and Emma went to their martial arts class at the YMCA. They were working their way through the various skills that originated as forms of self-defense. Emma planned to exercise extra hard today to work off all the calories she had ingested on her date. Staying in shape was an important part of her job but also a personal goal that she maintained so she could ace the annual physical fitness standards testing that her job required. She was proud of the fact that she often scored higher than some of her male counterparts. Just as important, being fit, both body and soul might someday mean the difference between life and death for herself or her partner when they were in the field.

Emma had challenged Jean to join her on Saturdays after she told Emma, that she believed a woman should be able to do more than just scream. Jean said she wanted to be a modern day warrior who could take care of herself if need be. Jean accepted the challenge and now they often made a day of it. After class, the women went to a favorite diner for a light snack, then decided to spend the rest of the afternoon shopping. They agreed that Emma needed to expand her footwear collection if she was going to date Peter. Wouldn't hurt to buy a pretty sundress for Sunday either! Emma couldn't remember the last time she had bought new clothes for herself. This was going to be an exciting weekend. Peter's entrance into her life was adding some extra zip to her zip a dee doo dah.

## CHAPTER 17

Alexander left Toronto, Canada early Friday morning. He returned home with great anticipation, anxious to begin preparations for his expected guest. His next elimination, Mr. Edward O. Jackson. He hummed as he taped tarps to the floors and walls and laid out his supplies so everything would be ready when needed. He continued to tweak and adjust the final scenario in his mind. Had he thought of every possibility? Everything that might go wrong? Did he miss anything? No, of course not, he was satisfied, it was perfect.

After a refreshing nap Alexander began composing his journal, *Adventures in Murder*. He found it quite therapeutic writing about himself. When he closed the journal, he was pleased with how well he was able to use words to express himself. Perhaps he should think about becoming a writer to supplement his income. That would be an easy way to make a living. Just sit in front of a computer and type words onto a pretend sheet of paper, how hard could that be? He had found it rejuvenating to record his thoughts and expand on his motivation. He felt blessed with his superior intellect and his unselfish commitment to ensure justice for all. The world would mourn his passing after they discovered and studied his journal. Perhaps it could be used as a textbook in a more enlightened world than the one he lived in at the moment.

When midnight came, he went out to begin his adventure. The pursuit and elimination of Edward Jackson had begun, or as Sherlock Holmes might have said, "the game's afoot".

Alexander stood in the shadows outside the Shamrock bar waiting for Jackson to leave. When he did appear, he was surrounded by several people who stood in the parking lot talking and laughing with him. They patted him on the back, shook his hand, then they all got into their respective cars and drove away. Alexander resigned himself that Jackson would live another day.

Alexander couldn't help but be distressed by what he had just witnessed. What did they have to laugh about? Alexander accepted that these evil doers could always justify their actions, they deceived everyone, including themselves but still, how could anyone befriend this remorseless wife-beating murderer?

They must all be evil, and in all likelihood, they should die as well. For now, he had to return home empty handed. Tomorrow he would have to examine Jackson's social media pages again. How ignorant these people were to disgorge all the minute details of their lives, informing the world where they were going and with whom. Fools! But thank God for fools, he reasoned. It made it easy for him to trace Jackson's movements, to know where he would be drinking tomorrow night so he could capture his prey and eliminate him forever.

The following evening, Alexander stood in the shadows outside a different bar. The Main Place on Alexander. He was waiting for Mr. Jackson to depart. It was almost two a.m. Sunday morning and Alexander was growing weary when he heard the doors open and saw Jackson walking out alone. Jackson appeared to have consumed too much alcohol and was having some difficulty locating his car in the dark parking lot behind the bar. A few seconds later he appeared to have fixed his sights on his vehicle and began approaching it, fumbling with his keys as he concentrated on locating the button to unlock the doors.

Alexander moved unnoticed behind him until he was close enough to press the chloroform soaked rag over his nose and mouth. Jackson gasped as he took in a deep breath, then collapsed into Alexander's arms.

Alexander had parked his car next to Jackson's allowing him to pivot around and open his passenger door then guide the unconscious man inside. He fastened the seatbelt around Jackson's body before closing the car door. He bent down to retrieve the keys and cap that had dropped on the ground. He walked around his car to the driver's door where he stood motionless, taking a long look around to assure himself no one was in the area before he got behind the wheel. In less than a minute they were gone.

Alexander drove to his house and into the seclusion of his garage. As soon as the overhead door closed, he drew in a deep breath of relief. He took a minute to enjoy the rush offered by his adventure. He felt overwhelming satisfaction with himself. He opened the passenger door to gaze at the unconscious man before he unfastened Jackson's seatbelt then half pulled and half dragged him out of the car. He hauled Jackson down the hallway and into the servant's quarters. Jackson was heavier than he had anticipated. Alexander was struggling as they moved through the small kitchen to where he finally deposited the body onto the floor of the bathroom.

Now Alexander could relax. He removed Jackson's jacket and emptied the pockets. He continued searching Jackson's clothes until he discovered his wallet. He confiscated all the cash before shoving it back into his pants pocket. Satisfied that he had removed everything useful, Alexander wrestled the man's unconscious body into the tub, posing it into a sitting position so it faced the drain. He made short work of attaching Jackson's arms and legs to the custom restraints he had fashioned for the task. When he finished, Jackson was secured inside the tub so he could not move when he regained consciousness. These special restraints Alexander devised wouldn't leave any marks on Jackson's body for the police to find.

Exhausted but triumphant, he waited. Alexander wanted to talk with Mr. Edward O. Jackson. Discuss his crime, let him know he was going to die, and why. He didn't have to wait long before his victim opened his bloodshot eyes.

"What the hell! Where am I? Who the fuck are you?" Jackson fought to regain consciousness while struggling to move his arms and legs.

Alexander watched with delight as Jackson thrashed around in the tub trying to get up, but his restraints held firm. Too soon for Alexander's liking, Jackson gave up fighting and settled down. It appeared he was trying to focus his alcohol addled brain into assessing the situation.

Alexander sat in the doorway and stared at the man, making no attempt to hide his enjoyment of the other's confusion. When Jackson settled down, Alexander began his interrogation, "I just want to know one thing Mr. Jackson. Why? Why did you kill your wife?"

The man blinked several times, first with surprise then anger as he glared at Alexander. "What the hell are you talking about? What the fuck is it to you, asshole? You're fuckin' playin' with fire, jackass!"

Alexander was undisturbed by the foul language. He understood it was the language the ignorant fall back on when they have nothing else. "Please calm down, Mr. Jackson. I'm trying to comprehend how you could love someone enough to marry them and then hate them enough to murder them."

Jackson's eyes darted around the room, coming back to rest on Alexander. "What the fuck are you talking about! What the hell's going on, hey... is this a joke? This is not funny guys, let me go! NOW!" He shouted at some unseen person behind Alexander.

"I assure you this is no joke, we are alone here, and you need to answer my questions. You are on trial for the murder of your wife. The court wants to know why you killed her."

"The court! What fuckin court? You crazy son of a bitch! Who are you and what fuckin loony bin did you escape from?" He paused, "okay, okay, this has gone far enough, why don't you be a nice little crazy person and let me go? I can pay you, I have money, is that what you want?"

Alexander struggled to remain calm after Jackson's insinuations that he was crazy. The very idea was beyond repulsive to Alexander; he was trembling with emotion as he fought for control. He had a mission and he intended to let nothing distract him. "Money? You think you can pay for your crime with money? That's your first mistake. All your money has been sequestered to cover court costs."

"Sequestered, what the hell does that mean?"

"It means that I have appropriated your money, seized your cash, you have no funds with which to negotiate. To put it in terms you understand, you cannot buy your way to freedom... this time."

"No, wait, I… I have more, much more, just take me to any ATM and I can get you all the money you want."

"No, that money belongs to your children. Her children, the ones who lost their mother because of your narcissistic, demented behavior. Unless you can give the court a satisfactory defense, you are going to be executed tonight, Mr. Jackson."

Alexander sat back as he watched panic begin to take over Jackson's thoughts. He knew Jackson was trying hard to find a satisfactory justification for his actions.

"You have no idea what a goddamn bitch she was to live with." he offered.

Alexander gave no acknowledgement to that defense.

"Damn it all, it's none of your fuckin' business."

"Is that the summation of your defense?"

"Yes. I mean no. Okay, the truth is, she was planning on leaving me. She was planning on taking my children away from me. Me! … I had no fuckin choice, I went there to stop her one way or the other. I couldn't let her walk out with everything I had worked my entire life for. Everything was mine, including her, I couldn't let anyone else have her. A man has to be a man, I couldn't let her win, you understand what I'm talking about, I gave her everything and she still wanted to fuckin' leave me."

When Jackson stopped talking, Alexander announced his decision. "The court finds you guilty as charged and I hereby sentence you to death. Prisoner to be executed without delay."

Jackson began to struggle again, thrashing about without success as he shouted at Alexander. "I'm gonna kill you, just like I did her, you crazy fuckin' bastard!"

Jackson continued ranting and struggling with his bindings while Alexander watched with fascination. He was imagining the taste of panic, the blood surging through Jackson's veins, combined with the excess alcohol and the effect of the chloroform. Yes, this was most satisfying watching this evil man suffering while he waited for his execution.

Alexander had found a switchblade in Jackson's pocket. He set aside the hunting knife he had planned to use, determining that this would be much better. Alexander stood up now and displayed the knife he was planning to use to execute him.

Edward Jackson recoiled in horror at the sight of his own knife. He stopped struggling. "No, no, please. You're fuckin' crazy. You can't kill me. You're not a real court! I don't want to die!"

Alexander struggled to control the rage he experienced every time Jackson referred to him as crazy. "Is that what she said to you before you ended her life? Was this the knife you used to kill her?"

"No, no, she didn't see me, I made it quick. She never saw it coming! I didn't want her to suffer, I really loved her. Please, please, I'll do anything you say. I'll give myself up, I'll confess if that's what you want. Just tell me what do you want!"

"I want you to pay for what you did to her, I want you to die the same way she did." Alexander walked closer to the tub. Moving behind Jackson, Alexander bent over and jammed the knife into the top of Jackson's thigh, taking care that the angle was correct so that it looked self-inflicted.

"Ahh!" Jackson screamed out in pain and fear, "What the fuck? You stabbed me... you crazy son of a bitch! I'm bleeding, you have to help me. Stop the bleeding."

Alexander felt a welcome rush of adrenaline. "No, that won't be necessary. I cut your femoral artery. You have less than four minutes before you bleed out and die. Time for you to think about what you did to the woman you say you loved and ask for God's forgiveness before he sends you straight to hell. Perhaps now you will understand how she felt when you left her to bleed to death!" Alexander sat back down to watch Jackson die.

Jackson continued to thrash and scream at him, but Alexander tuned it out. As he waited, he had time to ponder the large sum of money he had confiscated from Jackson's wallet. He knew Jackson was in the habit of carrying large amounts of cash to flash around. How predictable. Just another textbook way bullies used to feel powerful. Alexander was pleased when his social media search had revealed that Jackson was one of those people, and he called Alexander crazy! It was a bonus finding the switchblade. Alexander felt blessed. He was sure it was another sign that God was indeed on his side. He watched with high expectations, anticipating the thrill of watching Jackson as he died. He was looking forward to experiencing the same pleasure he had experienced when he observed the life leaving Max's body. He felt cheated when Jackson not only failed to ask God's forgiveness, but simply closed his eyes as he drifted off to Hell.

Well, he thought, easy come, easy go. Maybe next time. He still had a few chores left to do. First, he plugged the drain so he could remove the tube that was siphoning Jackson's blood into the plastic container. Once that was sealed, he estimated that he had collected almost a gallon of Jackson's blood. He removed the plug to allow the remaining blood to flow down the drain.

Next, he removed the bindings and left Jackson sitting upright, with legs outstretched, his clothing soaking up the remaining blood. He placed the knife into the lifeless hand and positioned the still pliable fingers around it before rigor made them too stiff to bend. He was satisfied that all the blood was contained and he didn't have any on himself.

Still, he planned on disposing of his clothing along with all the rest of the materials he had used. Next he laid plastic over the body in the tub and turned on the air conditioner he had installed over the toilet. Then he removed his gloves, closed and locked the door and went to bed.

It had been a long day and he was very tired. He would enjoy a good night's rest now that he had completed another mission. Too bad it was so late Sunday morning. He would have to get up soon to attend church.

He was in a good mood now that he had more money to donate to the church. He remembered that he would have to go to confession tomorrow. He wondered how he would phrase his confession so the priest would give him permission to take communion? It wasn't really murder; he was only enforcing the sentence handed down by the court. He would tell the priest he had to eliminate a rabid animal before it hurt anyone again. He knew that God would forgive him. After all, they were working together, he was proud that he had been assigned to do God's work.

## CHAPTER 18

It was a beautiful Sunday morning when Emma turned off East Avenue onto Vick Park A. She was looking for number Five. Peter lived on the corner in a large three story brick home that was built in the mid 1800's. She parked in the driveway that curved around his front yard, providing easy entry and exit onto Vick Park A. She parked under the same canopy that must have been used by the horse drawn carriages of aristocrats in years past. Oh, if houses could talk, Emma thought, as she gazed with admiration at the simple beauty of the architecture. She was sure this house would have many interesting secrets and stories to share.

She wondered which elite Rochesterians' had visited this same house in years past; perhaps Susan B. Anthony or Frederick Douglass. Or George Eastman? After all, Eastman's house was just down the road. Perhaps Henry Strong dined here, the gentleman for whom the Strong Memorial Hospital was named. He was Eastman's friend and also the first president of Eastman Kodak Company. She thought about Rochester's cultured and diverse history as she exited her car and walked to the front door. Before she could ring the doorbell, the door swung open and Peter stood there to greet her.

"Welcome Emma, I'm so pleased to have you visit my home." He reached for her hand in a welcoming gesture. She stepped inside where he took her coat and handed it to a woman he introduced as Mrs. Kleinman, his housekeeper.

He led Emma through the house to the back, where she stepped through French doors into a glass conservatory. The warmth of the sun shining through the glass enveloped her as she stepped into the room, much like stepping into a warm blanket on a cold winter's night. The combined scents of dirt mixed with the fragrance of the various plants and flowers, tickled her nostrils.

She could hear the faint sound of water falling onto stones. The illusion was complete with a dozen or so, colorful butterflies that flitted from one flower to the next in their quest for food. Emma felt a wave of peaceful serenity wash over her the instant she stepped into that amazing conservatory. A gentle tug on her hand brought her focus back to Peter.

"I had forgotten the overpowering effect this room can have on first time visitors," he said, as he led her down the path, toward the round table that was set up in the middle of the sculptured shrubs and gorgeous flowering plants.

"Peter, this room is so beautiful, so peaceful and serene. I feel like I've stepped out of reality into a world of fantasy."

"I'm glad you like it. I thought we'd eat in here."

"Yes, this room is wonderful, it's perfect for a picnic."

"Allow me to show you around, this is one of my favorite rooms. This and the library." Peter lead her around, showing her the dozens of delicate blooms and inviting seating areas that were scattered throughout the large space. Emma didn't recognize many of the plants, some of which had foliage more striking than the flowers themselves. It was obvious that Peter was enamored of the rarities he cultivated as he provided both the Latin and common names for several specimens as they walked passed them, one more lovely than the next. Emma knew she wouldn't remember any of this, except perhaps the rare orchid Anacamptis pyramidalis because she was able to visualize her grade school friend Anna Campis making pyramids. She chuckled out loud, repeating the name and sharing the visual with Peter.

"I can't even keep a cactus alive." she confessed.

"Don't feel bad about that, Emma, cacti aren't as easy to care for as people think!"

Peter picked up a small silver bell that rested on a potting table near the door and before the sound of the bell's delicate ring had faded, a tall, well-built gentleman walked into the room. " Are you ready for lunch, sir?"

"Yes, Gordon." Peter turned to Emma and made introductions. "Emma, this is Gordon Kleinman. He and his wife have been with me for years. Gordon, this is Miss Emma Mason."

They exchanged polite greetings. Emma noted that Gordon Kleinman had a slight German accent. He was a big man, tall and muscular but he moved with a practiced, effortless grace that was almost cat like, quick and smooth. Based on the fold of his clothing, she was sure he was armed. Perhaps, she thought, he was also a bodyguard. But why would Peter need an armed bodyguard in his own home?

"Gordon, would you please bring us some of your wife's fresh lemonade?"

"Certainly, sir." Gordon turned and took his leave.

"Peter, your house is so interesting, how long have you lived here?

"I've owned it for 6 years now."

"Do you know it's history?"

"I know some, I'm still researching it when I have time. It was built sometime in the 1840's. I bought it from a couple related to the Sibley family. They wanted to move to California to escape our cold winters. Would you be interested in a tour?"

"Absolutely! I love to explore old houses and imagine what it was like living in the 19th century. I especially love to see homes that have the original room decorations and furnishings from those bygone years. I think it's fascinating!"

"Excellent! That's how I feel as well, let's start with the library, it's my favorite room." Peter took her hand and led her out of the conservatory, down the hall, into a room filled with books from floor to ceiling. There was a ladder attached to a track that slid along the entire wall, allowing easy access to the upper shelves.

"Emma again felt herself surrounded by sights and smells that made her senses tingle. It was the sensation of knowledge that filled the room. Fiction and nonfiction, the classics as well as modern novels occupied the shelves.

"My God Peter, have you read all these books?"

"Not even close. Most of these books were left by the previous owners, but when I have time, I will slip one off the shelf to read. I discovered that many of them are first editions."

"That's very impressive! Perhaps I could borrow one or two sometime. I love to read."

"It would be my pleasure. But I have to warn you, I am a firm believer in the policies practiced by Benjamin Franklin when he started the Library Company for the purpose of lending valuable books to non-members. First you will have to offer some sort of collateral in case the books are never returned."

"Deal!" Emma was excited at the prospect, but wondered what type of collateral would be considered acceptable.

"Let's continue our tour, the next room is the downstairs sitting room."

It took them over an hour to tour the entire house. Emma wanted to see everything, including the attic and cellar that had not been updated like the rest of the house. These old homes were built with heavy beams that were twice the size of the ones used in current construction. She could see the skeleton or bones of the house in those untouched areas. She marveled at the workmanship and shared with Peter her wonder at how they were able to secure and install these heavy pieces of timber without the aid of modern machinery. Gordon located them about halfway through the tour and proffered the lemonade as she was admiring the leaded windows and beautiful hardwood floors of the upstairs sitting room. They had just left Peter's bedroom, which Emma realized she had taken more than a casual interest in. She had looked at the ceiling over his bed to see if he had mirrors installed. The next instant, she wondered why she cared, but was grateful to see a standard ceiling over his extra-large, four poster bed. There was a large flat screen television bolted to the opposite wall surrounded by a sophisticated entertainment system. Double doors led to his closet that was large enough to be another room and the bathroom was even larger. It had been renovated to incorporate modern conveniences into the old fashioned setting. The house was an amazing structure incorporating new and old with flawless perfection. Peter had refurbished some of the old furniture that had been left in the house when he took possession and he had integrated those to blend in with the newer pieces he owned. Most of the flooring had been salvaged and refinished with great care then waxed and polished to a bright shine to return its original luster. The area rugs had been cleaned and repaired where necessary and returned to their proper place. The wall hangings, paintings and decorations had been removed one by one to be repaired or refurbished before they were rehung allowing everything to blend together in seamless beauty. His taste was elegant with a delightful sense of style.

Emma listened with appreciation as Peter described the condition of the house when he bought it and how he had researched and agonized over each decision during the remodel and upgrade. "The hardest part," he said, "and the most expensive by far, was changing out the plumbing. What a nightmare! Contractors started in the basement and worked their way up to the bathrooms on the third floor. Replacing every single piece of plumbing, nothing had been worth salvaging. It had taken three years because they were only able to do one or two rooms at a time. While they were at it, they replaced and upgraded the heating unit, all the electric in the house and added a top of the line security system as they worked on the plumbing. The kitchen had been the hardest and would have been impossible if not for the kitchen in the Kleinman's quarters. There's a real advantage to having two kitchens in a house when you have to shut one down for weeks." He showed her everything but one area of the house which he referred to as the Kleinman's residence. Peter explained that their two floor apartment was sealed off from the main house except for the one entrance door off the main hallway on the first floor. They had their own private entrance on the outside that included a small screened porch that they used often on warm summer evenings.

When they returned to the conservatory, Gordon was waiting with their picnic lunch. They sat down as he removed the stainless steel covers that had kept their steaks warm. Large Caesar Salads and warm rolls were already on the table along with a pitcher of iced Lemonade.

Emma was famished because she had skipped breakfast. She picked up her fork and began enjoying the delicious meal. Once her appetite had been sated, she noticed with surprise that the ensuing silence while they ate had not been uncomfortable. She looked again at the beauty that surrounded her. "Peter, I am so impressed with how hard you've worked to make your house so relaxing and inviting. It's a remarkable old home, and I must add that this lunch is absolutely delicious. You are truly an amazing man. I was expecting sandwiches and snacks, not grilled steak and salad. It's far and above the best picnic I have ever attended, and Gordon broiled the steak to perfection!"

"Good to hear! I confess I'm pulling out all the stops trying to impress you! I'm happy to hear that I'm succeeding. Gordon's cooking was my secret weapon, not many people can resist. Wait till you taste dessert! His wife is a skilled baker and she's making Baked Alaska for us."

"Really? My mother made Baked Alaska a couple of times when we had company. I was young but I still remember that I loved it - the cold ice cream under the warm meringue topping. But I'm afraid I'm way too full from lunch to enjoy that now."

"No problem, we can go for a walk outside first, it's a beautiful sunny spring day, perfect for a stroll down East Avenue. I can recite some of the history as we walk along. It's really a very interesting street. In my opinion, I think it's the most beautiful and historic in the city."

"Yes, let's do that. A stroll down East Avenue sounds wonderful." They left the conservatory and walked back to the foyer. She saw Mrs. Kleinman holding her coat, and reached out to take it from her.

"Thank you, Mrs. Kleinman, you're very kind but I've got it."

Peter stepped in and took her coat and held it for her to slip into. Emma sighed and allowed Peter to help her, this time. They left the house and strolled out to the sidewalk. The bright sun made her long for sunglasses. She heard the birds singing and felt the breeze blowing butterfly kisses across her face. She inhaled the fragrance of the spring flowers that were just beginning their cycle of rebirth after long winter months of hiding from the cold. She felt Peter slip his hand into hers and she realized she liked the feel of it. He led her to the street corner where they turned right and began their stroll down historic East Avenue.

"This first house belongs to my neighbor, Mr. Wright. The house was built around the 1840's, same as mine. His grandfather bought it in the 1900's and his family has owned it for three generations. A number of these houses, however, have never changed hands and have been owned exclusively by the same family since they were built." Peter stopped and stared at his neighbor's house.

Emma looked in the same direction to see what had startled him. A man appeared on the side of the house. He smiled as he walked towards them.

Peter began introductions straightaway. "Emma, this is my neighbor, Mr. Alexander Wright. Alex, this is my friend, Emma Mason."

As Emma extended her hand, she thought she saw surprise register on Alexander's face, but it disappeared a split second later as he smiled and shook her hand.

"Honored to meet you, detective," he mumbled, then turned his attention back to Peter. "I was just coming to see you; I didn't realize you were entertaining. I wanted to return the money I borrowed last week." Alexander pulled an envelope out of his pocket and handed it to Peter as he continued. "Thanks a million, I really appreciated it."

"No problem." Peter slipped the envelope into his pocket. "That's what friends are for. Glad I could help. I was just giving Emma a tour of the neighborhood, she likes these old mansions. Come to think of it, yours may be even older than mine. Would you mind showing Emma around?"

Again, Emma thought she saw a look of surprise, or was it fear, that was replaced in the blink of the eye, with a cordial smile.

"It would be my pleasure, follow me." Alexander led the way to the stairs of the front porch. "We'll enter through the front so you can appreciate this beautiful porch. As you can see, it wraps around my home on both sides." As they climbed the stairs he continued, "I consumed many carefree hours playing on this porch when I was a young boy. My parents sat in these chairs to relax, read the newspaper and converse with neighbors as they walked by, taking their evening strolls or exercising their dogs."

Once inside the home, they entered a glass vestibule, then a large open foyer. From there, Alexander lead them into an elegant living room featuring a very large brick fireplace. They walked through the living room, past large wooden pocket doors to enter the formal dining room.

Emma thought it strange that the table was arranged with three place settings displayed, one at each end of the long table, and one in the middle. The only one that had been disturbed was the one in the middle. The end ones appeared to be abandoned and covered in dust.

"I'm sorry I can't show you the upstairs. My parents died there. They were murdered and I haven't used those rooms since. This is my main living area. The library, kitchen, and baths are all this way." When they reached the kitchen, Emma noted there were two closed doors in the corner. The one on the back wall had windows and she could see that it led into the small backyard where she could see the back of Peter's house.

"Where does this door lead?" she pointed to the solid door on the inside wall.

"That opens into a breezeway that leads to the garage, the basement and the servants' quarters. But we'll have to see that area another time. I don't mean to be rude, but I have an appointment in 30 minutes and I'll need to leave soon or I'll be late."

"Of course, I know the way out, thanks for the tour Alex."

On their way out, they passed a wide curved staircase leading to the bedrooms on the second floor, then two large doors off the hallway on their left.

Emma paused, "Peter, what's behind these doors?"

"That was his father's study. I think Alexander uses it as his study now. Here we go, watch your step going down the stairs."

Emma's instincts were tingling again. She had a growing uneasiness in her stomach that she could not shake. Once they were outside on the public sidewalk, she stopped to question Peter.

"Peter, how did your neighbor know I was a detective?"

"Oh, he was with me when I spotted your medallion. In fact, he was the one that suggested the inscription. He said the jeweler was a friend of his father's. I'm embarrassed to admit, he gave me a break on the price and rushed it so I would have it in time for our date. Alexander brought it over to me that afternoon."

"What do you know about the murder of his parents? Was he a suspect?"

"No, he was at College when it happened. Police confirmed he was in classes the entire day. It happened a few years after I moved here. It was pretty brutal. Alex found them the next day when he came home for the weekend. I don't think he's recovered yet, but he's working through it. The police caught the man who did it. They even got a confession, but when they got to court, the confession was tossed, and they couldn't make the charges stick without it. The guy walked and that's when Alex had his breakdown. He was in a mental hospital for months, I looked after his house while he was gone. I really feel sorry for the guy. He never married and he was devoted to his parents - especially his mother. He told me they were very close. The whole thing was devastating." He paused, "Let's change the subject. We'll finish our walk and then go home and enjoy that Baked Alaska."

"You're right, it's my day off so let's enjoy the afternoon and no more talk about work, yours or mine."

"That's the second best offer I've had today, it's a deal!" Peter slipped his hand back into hers to continue their walk. It was two hours before they returned to the conservatory. Peter rang the little silver bell and Gordon appeared. Peter informed him they were ready for dessert.

It was served 30 minutes later, the meringue still warm from the oven and the ice cream soft but still cold, setting on a heavenly base of Angel food cake. It was perfect, thought Emma, even more delectable than she remembered.

Peter walked Emma out to her car and again he held her shoulders like he had the other night, pulled her close to brush his lips gently across hers. She felt herself again shivering with pleasure. Peter slipped his arms around her and pulled her in for a deep kiss that sent those same feelings of desire throughout her entire body. She closed her eyes, returning his kiss with a hunger that surprised her. Suddenly he stopped, then pulled away from her, holding her at arm's length.

"Whoa, you take my breath away Emma Mason. I'm sorry if I, if you, I mean if I have offended you in any way. I didn't mean to be so forward, I apologize."

Emma stepped back to catch her breath. "Oh, I understand, I mean, hmm, no need to apologize Peter." She pulled her car keys from her coat pocket. "I have to go. Thank you for an amazing afternoon." Emma turned and climbed into her car, trying to be more graceful than she felt. She clicked the seat belt closed, turned the key and started the engine. Rolling down the driver's window, she looked at Peter.

He was staring at her like a child caught with his hand in the cookie jar. He looked so uncomfortable and unsure of himself that she had to laugh. He smiled at her when she laughed, relief showing all over his face.

"Good-bye for now Emma Mason, I'll be in touch."

"Looking forward to it Peter Hartman."

She pulled out of his driveway and headed home. My life sure is getting exciting, she thought. Wait until Jean hears about our picnic, right in his very own indoor park. Emma wondered how long she would be home before Jean would be at her door pestering her with questions. She laughed at the thought but the truth was she was anxious to tell her all about it. Looking down, she noticed the dashboard clock read 5:45. She was stunned. Where did the day go? It's already dinner time and I've just finished lunch!

Well, she had to admit, Mr. Peter Hartman was, without question, the most interesting man she had ever met. Still she had those annoying red flags flying around in the back recesses of her mind. Was he also a dangerous one? Did he have an ulterior motive for pursuing her? Why would a man like him be interested in a woman like her? The suspicious cop and the anxious romantic fought with each other, searching for answers. Never had she experienced such indecision or exhilaration over her love life. She had no idea where it was going, but she already knew that the heat and intensity would be unlike anything she had ever experienced. She had to admit she was looking forward to discovering more about him and perhaps about herself as well.

## CHAPTER 19

Alexander hurried to get his car keys. He needed to leave his home to verify the appointment he'd invented so he didn't have to show her the rest of the house. He had to think fast when the detective asked what was behind the door. He pictured her face if he had confessed. 'Just a dead body in the bathtub!' He chuckled at the image. Damn it all, why didn't Peter warn him that he was entertaining *her*? Thank God they didn't come in the side door. He thought Emma may have been able to smell the body through the two locked doors and the plastic cover. The very thought made him shiver, then he realized how exciting it had been. The adrenalin was pumping and he relished the feeling of imminent danger. Reminded him of the Edgar Allen Poe story, *The Tell-Tale Heart*, but that was about a man who was mad. Or was it the act of killing that had driven him mad? Well, there was no comparison, he was enjoying his new line of work. It certainly

199

was not driving him mad. Just the opposite, it was enabling him to live his life with purpose and direction. He smiled as he climbed into his car. Flashes of his  hospital experience crashed like lightning into his thoughts. Those Doctors were all wrong about him. He knew the truth. They were the ones with the problem. If it weren't for them, most of his problems would have gone away, but they continued prodding and probing, keeping his wounds open and unbearably painful. All they did was talk and ask ridiculous questions, then shove those dreadful pills down his throat. Thank God they had books in the hospital. He spent hours reading the classics. Poe was one of his favorite authors. Alexander believed that all the creative writers were in the past. Writers that could fabricate intricate and imaginative story lines like Poe and Doyle. He was convinced the world would never be entertained by such talented authors again.

Alexander backed his car out onto the street and headed towards Peter and Emma. He beeped the horn as he passed, then made a series of right hand turns, allowing him to return to his own driveway. He'd be safe once he pulled into the garage and the overhead door closed behind him.

Now he could resume his planned activities. He rounded up clothing similar in style and color to what Mr. Jackson was wearing and put them on. Stuffing Jackson's jacket and hat into a nondescript bag, he walked out his front door.

After checking to make sure Peter and Emma were out of sight, he set out walking in the opposite direction, to the corner of Vick Park A. He turned the corner and zig zagged two more blocks before boarding a city bus that would take him to Alexander Street to retrieve Jackson's car from the bar's parking lot.

Alexander enjoyed riding the bus with all the plebeians because these people seldom paid any attention to their fellow passengers. He imagined he was invisible to them, as he listened in on their phone conversations. He watched them talking and interacting, not caring what was discussed or how much of themselves they gave away. He suspected that a couple young thugs were taking undue interest in him, but they were distracted when three young girls boarded. He wondered if these boys might end up on his radar in the future. He already knew he would enjoy eliminating them, especially the one that wore his hat backwards and his pants down around his hips. The boy should be ashamed to go out in public dressed like that. His mother must be so proud. Alexander snickered to himself. The other wasn't much better. His pants weren't falling off, but he was covered in tattoos and piercings. Alexander was unwilling to imagine what other horrors were inflicted on the covered parts of his body. He was pleased that the young girls exhibited no interest in them. They selected seats near the front of the bus, well away from the young thugs.

Alexander was torn when his stop came and he had to disembark. He so enjoyed observing his fellow passengers, but it was time to leave this particular fishbowl. He collected his things and pulled the cord. He was only a few blocks from the bar when he stepped off the bus wearing Jackson's hat and jacket. Slipping on a pair of large sunglasses, he began walking toward the bar and Jackson's car. Once at the vehicle, he slipped on a pair of clear plastic gloves, then unlocked Jackson's car and slipped in. He adjusted the seat and mirror, making sure to note where they were so he could return everything to its proper place. He wasn't about to let them trip him up on such a small detail.

He drove the car to the park where he knew the cameras would be active. He parked, then readjusted everything before he got out and locked the doors. He puzzled at his sudden impulse to look up at the camera. Alexander put it down to nerves and fought the urge. Taking his time, he walked into the woods, keeping his back to the cameras. When he was sure he was unobserved by others in the park, he removed the hat and jacket and returned them to the bag. He continued walking until he reached the paved bicycle path along the Genesee river. Now he removed his gloves and sunglasses and put them into his pocket. He walked at a brisk pace, along the path until he crossed the Court Street bridge to utilize a different bus route.

He was looking forward to this bus ride. It would take longer and it traveled through several undesirable neighborhoods so he would have more time to observe the seedy travelers that accompanied him. It was necessary to transfer once downtown in order to catch a bus going back to his East Avenue neighborhood. He chose to get off the bus a few blocks from home so none of his neighbors would observe him disembarking. While he walked the remainder of the distance home, he was looking forward to enjoying a nice cup of hot tea. He had to wait until nightfall before he would be able to move the body to the park.

Alexander was very pleased with his progress so far. Everything was going according to plan. He took a steak out of the freezer. Tonight he would enjoy a well-deserved dinner to celebrate. Maybe even a quick nap while the steak thawed. He would need all his faculties tonight.

His alarm sounded at 3 am Monday morning, but Alexander was already awake and busy checking to make sure the windows in the servants' quarters remained light tight so no one would see the lights while he worked. Once he was assured that everything was still secure, he turned on the lights in the kitchen, unlocked the door to the windowless bathroom and entered. In addition to plastic gloves, he wore dark colored, disposable hooded coveralls to protect his identity in case he was seen during his adventure.

The room was very cold. The air conditioner he secured on the tank of the toilet after removing the lid was working hard, maintaining a temperature in the forties. He hoped the cold air would disguise the actual time of death from early Sunday morning to late Sunday afternoon. He removed the plastic covering from over the body and spread it on top of the tarp covering the floor.

Wresting the body from the tub, he laid it on the plastic then folded and secured the plastic around the ends with tape. He removed and carefully folded the tarps from the walls. He then lifted the gallon container of Jackson's blood and the bag containing his hat, jacket and the knife that he had wrapped separately to secure the blood and fingerprint evidence. He carried these to his car and loaded them safely inside before returning to remove Jackson's body. Alexander was surprised how light the body was now that most of the blood had been drained. Of course, Jackson was an athlete, so he was lean to begin with, but regardless, it was going to be easier than he thought to carry the body into the woods.

Alexander relaxed once he was on the road. He knew where he was going because he was familiar with this area along the Genesee River. He played there as a boy and knew all the hidden entrances and exits, the location of the cameras in the parking areas and all the private roads that rail workers used to maintain the tracks that ran along the river. He was soon driving on one of those dirt roads, traveling until he was out of sight of any homes. He parked his car at the end of the road, alongside the tracks, where he couldn't be observed. He donned a low beam headlamp he'd customized with electrical tape so only a miniscule beam of light shone through, pointed at the ground.

Wearing latex gloves, Alexander tied the bag containing all of Jackson's belongings to his belt. He then picked up the body, and with some difficulty was able to position it over his right shoulder. With his left hand, he grabbed the container of blood by its handle and started walking along the railroad tracks watching for the dirt path he was seeking.

Once he turned down that side trail, he moved at a steady pace, away from the tracks and deeper into the woods. He navigated the narrow path with care. He needed to rest once and sat down on a large tree trunk that had fallen alongside the trail. As he rested, he listened for any sound that might indicate human intervention, but heard only the flowing river and the faint sound of a few lone cars navigating the distant highway.

He continued moving through the darkness until he arrived at the large maple tree he had selected. He set Jackson's body down against a large uprooted tree. Returning to the maple, he took the container of blood and poured it into the dirt about a foot and a half away from the tree. He waited for the blood to soak into the ground. While he waited, he returned to the body and went through the process of unwrapping it before he carried it over to the maple tree. He placed it in a sitting position against the tree with Jackson's cut leg positioned over the bloodied earth.

He removed the bloody knife from the sealed bag and slipped it back into Jackson's hand. Satisfied, he placed Jackson's car keys into the pocket of his jacket and hung it on a branch of the tree, just over Jackson's head. After using a baby wipe to clean the inside, he placed the hat on Jackson's head and it was done. The scene was set and Alexander had to admit, it was perfect.

He stepped back to admire his work, much like an artist would check his completed work just one more time before the public unveiling.

Satisfied, Alexander returned to fold the empty piece of plastic so all the excess blood was on the inside, then put everything on top and folded it again, securing it with tape so all the items were contained in one easy to carry bundle. Last, he found a sturdy broken limb from a nearby shrub and used it to brush the ground, erasing all evidence of his presence. He continued to sweep the ground as he backed his way down the narrow path using his low beam flashlight directed at the ground to ensure that he did not miss anything. He didn't plan to leave any clues that the police could discover, unraveling all his hard work. As he reached the railroad tracks, he was satisfied they would find no imprints suitable for casting. At that point, he removed his coveralls, turned them inside out, and added them to his bundle.

When he returned to his car, only the faintest of stars shown in the sky. He removed his headlamp and tossed it into the footwell on the passenger side of the car. He then extracted a pair of throwaway shoes from the trunk, and exchanged them with the disposable tennis shoes he purchased in Toronto. He did the same with the latex gloves, pulling on a clean pair to finish the job. He would have to dispose of all these items, even the branch he used to cover his tracks. He would not let anything trip him up. He would not leave anything to chance. He spread out a second, clean piece of plastic and loaded everything into it, wrapped it and placed it into the trunk.

When he started his car, he saw that it was 4:25 am and was pleased that his evening had gone so smooth. He still had time before the sun rose, to drive west toward the suburb of Parma, to the town's landfill before it opened, to dispose of the evidence. He knew they had not installed cameras and there was a deserted road behind the landfill where he could park undetected.

It was still dark when he parked and opened his trunk. He carried his bundle of evidence a short distance to a small pile of abandoned trash at the edge of the landfill. He opened the two pieces of plastic and unceremoniously shook them out, sending evidence in all directions. He picked up the container that held the blood, filled it with dirt, then jumped up and down on it half a dozen times until it cracked in several places. He threw it as hard as he could into a different pile of trash. Jamming the plastic he had used to wrap the body, under yet another pile of trash, and the tarps under yet another. He couldn't help but smile at his cleverness - everything hidden in plain sight, never to be found. He turned to walk back to his car, on the way, he removed his gloves and tossed first one then the other in different directions. He pulled his expensive footwear from the passenger seat and sat down with the door open, exchanging them with the second pair of throwaways on his feet. He tossed those shoes in different directions as well. He was thoroughly enjoying himself, having great fun tossing everything indiscriminately in all directions.

As he drove back toward the city, the sun was just beginning to peek out and was soon in its full glory. Fingers of radiant light streamed out from breaks in the clouds to touch the morning dew, creating a sparkling illusion of shimmering beauty on the ground. Alexander accepted it as a thank you from God for the successful completion of his task. It was God's way of saying, "well done."

Alexander now drove his car southeast of town, to a dealership in the nearby village of Victor. He had made an appointment to have his car detailed. Cleaning it from top to bottom would ensure that no trace of last night's activities remained. Once that was completed, he could drive home and into his garage without worrying about dropping bits or pieces of trace evidence from his car or tires onto his garage floor. He congratulated himself on having thought of everything.

It was late morning when he arrived home. He went to the bathroom and filled the bloody bathtub with water, leaving enough room to allow him to add three bottles of heavy duty bleach. That should remove any DNA evidence. He planned to let that set for an hour, then let it drain down into the pipes to remove all traces of Jackson's blood. While he waited, he scrubbed down the rest of the bathroom and put everything away. He pulled the plug out of the tub and watched the water drain, removing all vestige of the night's activities. He sprinkled cleanser into the tub and scrubbed every inch until he was positive the tub was free of all evidence. When he was done, the entire bathroom shone like a photo from Better Homes and Gardens. He removed the air conditioner from the room and replaced the lid on the toilet tank. The last thing he did was remove and refold the heavy sheets he had doubled and attached to the windows. One last look to insure that everything was back to normal. He walked out and locked all the doors.

After a short nap, Alexander thought about all the work that had gone into Jackson's elimination and how little had been needed for Maxwell's. He knew it was up to him to plan these eliminations better. He needed to take into account how much effort would be needed to erase his participation from these crimes. All things considered though, he was pleased that he had been able to eliminate another murderer that the law failed to punish for his crime. He hoped it would be days before the body was discovered in the woods.

He fixed himself a big breakfast of bacon, eggs, toast and coffee, then he sat back in his favorite velvet-upholstered chair, relaxed and happy. Life was good again. He felt his parents' approval, and it meant everything to him that they were proud of him for helping the police bring these murderers to justice. He would be sure to mention that in his journal. He would have tomorrow to work on that, today he would enjoy his success, along with a well-earned rest. Even God rested on the 7th day.

Tomorrow he would begin to search for the next despicable murderer that needed to be eliminated from this world.

## CHAPTER 20

It was Emma's habit to arrive at work early on Monday mornings to chat with the officers assigned to weekend duty. She stopped to chat with each one in her unit, gathering reports as she went. She liked to get their personal thoughts on the events covered in their written accounts and use those observations to paint a complete picture.

She was still walking on air, feeling amazing after her eventful weekend activities. She displayed a cheerful grin as she walked through the station carrying a large gourmet coffee purchased from her favorite coffee shop.

Once in her office, she sat down to examine the reports. As she read, she played with the medal around her neck, sliding it back and forth across the chain. She had debated wearing it, but decided that it couldn't hurt and it might help. In reality perhaps she wanted to believe in the ability of these so called Patron

Saints to protect the people who wore their medallions. She admitted to herself it was just foolish superstition but the medal was beautiful and it's the thought that counts. It's a sign that someone cared. She could believe in that at least.

Emma was just finishing with the weekend reports when Brett's tall, lanky frame filled her doorway. He was one of Jack's officers, delivering the report on the boys from Friday.

Emma liked Brett. He was an easy-going guy. Affable and chatty. Often fooling people into thinking he wasn't paying attention, but he didn't miss a trick. Jack often relied on Brett's keen observations of the people they interviewed, not for the words they used, but the meaning behind those words. Brett was skilled at reading body language and understanding motivation. Brett also enjoyed playing practical jokes on members of the department now and again but they were never mean-spirited and generally made everyone laugh, including the target. To his credit, he never crossed the line, and was well liked by his fellow officers.

"Here's the paperwork as promised."

"Thanks Brett, how's your wife?"

"Oh, Barb's doing well. Thanks for asking. We've got a long weekend coming up. We're taking Barb's mother camping with us to a place called Whiskey Creek. We're both looking forward to it. We all enjoy the outdoors this time of year."

"Your Mother-in-law is going camping with you? Oh, I get it, you're joking. Good one! That's pretty funny." She started to laugh out loud.

"No! It's no joke. I'm serious. I'm one of those lucky people, my Mother-in-law is one of the good ones. Could be because she lives in Seattle and we only see her once or twice a year. But we both enjoy her visits. No joke." He appeared anxious for Emma to believe him.

"Sounds great then! I hope you enjoy your getaway." Emma hoped to cover her faux-pas. "Thanks for hand delivering this report Brett."

"You got it. By the way, Jack said to tell you it was a good call not to bet against Anne, they are now the proud owners of two rescue mutts."

Emma heard him laughing as he turned and walked out of her office. She still wasn't sure if he was serious or not and knowing Brett she never would be.

The report indicated that the facts, as reported by the boys, lined up with the footprint evidence but did not coincide with suicide. Instead, this new evidence indicated that the body was moved into position after death in an effort to make it appear to be a suicide.

After adding this information to her board Emma tried to find any thread that she had overlooked, any clue she had missed. She dialed Mitch's extension and asked him to join her.

Mitch came in carrying a half eaten donut, as usual. This time it was chocolate glazed with colorful sprinkles, at least that was what remained of the half he hadn't eaten.

"Morning Emma, hope you don't mind if I eat my breakfast while we talk. I just got in.

"No problem, what kind of police station would we be if somebody wasn't eating a donut?"

"I'm taking the hit for the team." He stood up and saluted as he took another big bite then sat back down on the corner of her desk. He leaned in close and whispered, "So… tell me, how did your date go? Anything interesting come up?" He laughed at his little pun.

"To answer your first question, I had a very nice  weekend. I enjoyed my date and none of your business on your second question. Peter was a complete gentleman, and I have to say, he's a very interesting man. But I called you in to talk about our case. It's official, Jacks latest report categorized it as a homicide."

Emma handed Jacks report to Mitch, "I added this info to the board and hit a dead end. I'm hoping you might have another angle. We need a lead, a direction, I don't see anything we overlooked."

Mitch slid off her desk to sit in the one guest chair in Emma's office. He leaned back. Sipping his coffee between the last bites of donut, he studied the murder board. "By the way," he said, "I was playing with my home computer last night and I ran a check on Peter Hartman Enterprises. It's been very successful over the years and he is listed as sole owner, that would make him a very, very rich man."

"What? You did what? Why would you do that, Mitch?"

"Because you're my partner Emma, and I promised to watch your back. That doesn't end when we go home. I take my responsibilities very seriously and something just doesn't feel right about the guy... I just don't want you to be a *stupmitten*, I want you to be careful. Frankly I'm surprised you didn't run a check on him yourself."

"Mitch, my personal life is just that, personal. And what the hell is a stupmitten?

"Stupid and smitten at the same time, that's a bad combination."

Emma moaned, "Okay partner, listen up, I'm a grown woman and you do not have to watch my back when we are not at work. I can't believe th…'

"Emma, the last thing I ever want to do is upset you, but let me finish. I think you need to know what I discovered. I'll back off, but there's more. Peter has enemies, dangerous ones. There was an attempt on his life six years ago in New York City. Peter was shot, almost died. The police identified the perpetrator. A professional hitman for hire. Before they could bring him in for questioning, his body was found tied to the piling of an abandoned pier. At least enough of his body so they could ID him. There were small cuts in his legs that attracted crabs and other carnivorous marine life. He was being eaten alive before he finally drowned when the tide came in. He was gagged, so no one would have heard him screaming. It was a horrific death. No suspects were ever apprehended."

Emma shuddered. Her imagination conjured up images of the horrible death.

"Was Peter a suspect?"

"No, not directly. He had been shot the day before and was in the hospital recovering from surgery to remove the bullet." Mitch slid his feet off her desk and stood to leave.

"Wait Mitch, you stay here, see what you can come up with. I'm going out. I'll let you know when I get back." Emma walked out of her office. She felt like she'd been sucker punched and she needed time to think. A history like that would explain the need for Peter to have a bodyguard, and even the private dining room at the restaurant. Perhaps he was not as smitten as she thought, perhaps he was just being careful. Mitch had given her a lot to think about, and he was right about one thing, she needed to take a step back and be more cautious. Peter might be as dangerous as his enemies.

She headed to the gym in the basement. She needed to tame her emotions. She worked out until her energy was spent and her thoughts had returned to the Maxwell case. Feeling refreshed, she cleaned up and went back to her office. Mitch was gone. Sipping cold coffee, she stared at her murder board hoping something would jump out at her. Maybe they should go back to Maxwell's residence and interview more of the people who lived there. There's got to be a clue somewhere. Emma put in a call to Mitch and was told that he'd been called out on another case. A body had been found in the woods that morning by an older couple taking a walk, a possible suicide.

Emma walked out of her office and stepped into the uniformed officers break room. She spotted officer Geraci just getting up to leave.

"Break over, officer?"

"Yes ma'am, I was just going back to work."

"Good. Sign out so you can accompany me to do some follow-up interviews. We'll be at 441 Meigs Street. Meet me in the garage in fifteen."

"Yes ma'am, I'll be there."

Emma was glad to have this chance to work with officer Geraci. He was the most recent recruit to her unit. She thought he had shown potential. This would give her an opportunity to evaluate him further. Wouldn't hurt to toss him a bit of field experience, maybe give him the lead on one of the interviews.

A light rain was falling as they arrived at the former residence of Luther Maxwell. It was a typical spring day in Rochester. Warm sunshine appeared and disappeared as rain clouds raced across the sky forcing the sun into a game of peek-a-boo. They rang buzzers one at a time until an attractive young blonde woman appeared at the door. Emma held up her badge and identified herself and officer Geraci "We'd like to ask you a couple of questions."

"Look, I'm running late. I bartend at the Brick and Nail and I'm scheduled to work the early shift. Crazy boss man had me work late last night and now I have to go in early today to fill in. When is a girl supposed to get her beauty sleep? Acts like I wake up this gorgeous. Doesn't understand it takes time to put myself together."

Emma pulled out her recorder and let her finger hover over the record button. "May I record our conversation?"

"Depends. How long are we going to be and what's this about?"

"Just a couple of minutes. It's about a former neighbor of yours, Luther Maxwell"

"Okay, no problem, but please, make it quick like a bunny."

Emma turned on her recorder. "May 26, at 10:35 am. Luther Maxwell case. Would you please state your name and address for the record?"

"Rose Marie Pacelli. Four forty-one Meigs, apartment 4."

"How well did you know Luther Maxwell?"

"He was my neighbor. I heard the poor guy was dead. Is that right? Shot through the heart is what I heard."

"He is deceased. How well did you know Mr. Maxwell?"

"Well, I saw him at the bar more than I saw him here." She looked at officer Geraci. "Say, you're a looker, ever get up this way, come and see me at the Brick and Nail, I'm there most weekends."

Officer Geraci cleared his throat then turned his head and glanced out toward the road, giving it a quick sweep before resting his gaze once again on their witness.

Emma continued, "Could you describe Luther Maxwell's activities? How often he frequented the bar?"

"Yes, of course. He lived in the little apartment on the first floor. Just nodded when I saw him here, but he would come into the bar two, three times a week. Boy oh boy, could he talk when he was drinkin', but I didn't mind 'cause he was a good tipper."

"Oh, what did he talk about when you saw him at the bar?"

"I don't know, I just pretended to listen 'cause, like I said, he was a good tipper. But the last time I saw him he was going on about a new friend he had. Some guy that gave him a ride home from court a couple weeks ago."

"Did you know why Maxwell was in court?"

"Nah, but he did say his new friend had a nice car, so I told him to bring him in so's I could meet him, he said he would, but never did."

"Did he happen to mention his friend's name?"

Rose Marie thought a moment, "I think he did, but I don't remember, if I think of it I could call you, or you could come visit me again, officer Geraci." She flashed an enticing smile at the officer.

"Have you ever heard him mention a Mr. Reed?" Emma continued.

"Oh sure, I know Reed. He came in with Luther once in a while. He's a harmless drunk, it wasn't him, I'm pretty sure Reed drives an old truck."

Emma thanked her and gave Rose Marie her card. "Please call me if you think of anything else. Do you know if there are any other residents home today?"

"Everyone's gone to work. Maybe if you come back after 6 you would find more people home." Her eyes looked over at officer Geraci's face and drifted down his frame and back up again. "Bye, officer Geraci." She grinned as she closed the door and went back up to her apartment.

Emma clicked off her recorder. "Well, that was interesting, wouldn't you agree, officer 'good lookin'?"

Geraci faked a cough. "She appeared to be a credible witness, honest and cooperative."

"And did you also notice that she was flirting with you officer?"

"No, ma'am, hmmm, I mean, yes ma'am."

"That's a relief, I would have to wonder about your powers of observation if you had missed those moves. Looks like that's all we can do here, let's go."

"If you would like me to do a follow-up interview with this witness, I'd be happy to volunteer."

"Thank you again officer. I do appreciate your unselfish dedication to the job."

They were on their way back to the station when Emma's cell phone rang. She pushed the answer button and put it on speaker. "Mason here, with officer Geraci."

"Emma, it's Mitch. I think you should come out here and look at this body. Doc MacGee is on scene and he agrees. How fast can you get here?"

"Where are you?"

"Genesee Valley Park. The wooded section furthest back, between the golf course and the railroad tracks that run along the river."

"We're only a few blocks away. Be there in ten."

"Great! We'll hold the scene until you get here. Park in the back lot, you'll see our cars."

"Copy that."

Minutes later, Emma and officer Geraci were walking along the dirt path, using care to avoid evidence markers along the way. Mitch waved when he spotted them.

"Over here Emma! Glad you were so close. My IAFIS screen shows this is the body of Edward O. Jackson. He's famous for playing professional tennis. He was tried for murdering his wife in California, was found not guilty and freed. That's his jacket, hanging from the tree limb, keys in the pocket, no sign of a struggle, phone, watch, wallet all here. Older couple standing over there with officer Carris called 911 when they saw the body. They were taking their morning exercise and took this shortcut to get to the river. Lucky for us or no telling when we would have found the body. Give her your report first Doc."

"Alright Mitch. This gentleman appears to have died from exsanguination. Judging from the cut in his leg and all the blood he sliced the femoral artery. He would have bled out in minutes. From all the blood in the ground under his leg, it would appear to have happened here. The soil is quite saturated. His hand is still wrapped around the knife. TOD looks like less than 24 hours but I will have to get the body back to the morgue to confirm."

"Sounds open and shut. Why did you want me here?"

"Well, a couple of things are bothering me. A quick examination of the bottom of his shoes doesn't show any evidence of him having walked in here on his own. In addition, despite the fact that he was a right-handed tennis player, he was in fact, a lefty in almost everything else. His father thought being a lefty would be a disadvantage in tennis, so he taught him to play using his right hand. That came out at the murder trial. The knife is in his right hand. Also, a quick check of his pockets didn't turn up any cash and he was known for carrying large amounts of it. Last point, and this is why I wanted you here, this reminds me of the Maxwell case. A known perpetrator dead under suspicious circumstances made to look like a suicide and only thing missing appears to be the cash."

"Impressive, Mitch!" Emma paused for a minute while she assembled all of Mitch's observations. She walked around looking at the body, then the ground. "I agree. It looks like someone went to a lot of trouble setting the stage to misdirect us. Good chance it's linked with the Maxwell case. That means we may be investigating a serial killer."

"Pardon me, ma'am, but it might also be a vigilante killing." officer Geraci chimed in. "It could be that you're dealing with a person obsessed with rectifying justice failed. Both your victims were killers themselves."

"That's an interesting observation Geraci. You may have hit on a possible motive." She took a few steps backward while she continued to examine the scene.

"Mitch, let's be careful to cover all our bases. Find out where Jackson was the last few days of his life. Check his phone, get Jack's unit in here to go over the scene. Doc have your entomologist take samples of the ground around and under the body to help with the TOD. Have him take a look at the shoes and verify Mitch's observations. Officer Geraci, interview the couple that found the body then let them go. Talk to officer Carris first to see what he has. Then catch up with me in the parking lot. Let's keep this new angle under wraps from the press, they are going to be all over this story. We want the killer to think we bought the suicide. Mitch, toss me Jackson's keys and I'll see if his car is one of those parked in the lot. If it is, I'll leave Geraci with the car until Jack's unit can process it. Oh, check with Park maintenance and see if those cameras covering the lot are working. If they are, get the feed for the last two days.

226

I'll meet you back at headquarters. That will give me time to get a warrant for Jackson's home. Thanks and good work everyone."

## CHAPTER 21

Emma was busy organizing her second murder board and timeline when Mitch walked in eating a steaming hot dog dripping with hot sauce.

"Lunch. I stopped at the food cart on my way in."

"Fine, have a seat."

"Emma, about this morning, I'm sorry I upset you, but I… you needed to know what…"

"Forget it Mitch, you were right to tell me what you uncovered. I'm just not comfortable with your decision to look at

Peter. Let's stick to work. We have more important things to deal with right now. What have you got so far? No, wait, one new item I uncovered on the Maxwell case this morning. Geraci and I interviewed another tenant at his address. A Miss Rose Marie Pacelli. She remembered that Maxwell had acquired a new friend a week or so before he died. Friend drove a nice car. I added it to the board. That could be the man we're looking for."

"Great, did you get a name?"

"No, that would be way too easy!"

Emma relaxed as they settled into the comfortable conversation that defined their successful working relationship. "Now what have you got from this morning?"

Mitch devoured the remaining bit of hot dog and wiped his mouth. "Jack's unit's still working the scene. Doc's got the body in the morgue and the car you discovered in the lot was towed to impound for processing. Did you find anything in the car?"

"No, it was clean as far as I could tell. I'm hoping Jack 's unit will find something."

Mitch pulled out his notebook and started reading from his notes. "I found interesting footage from the camera feeds in the parking lot. Sunday afternoon, around 2:45 pm Jackson's car pulled in and parked. A man that looks like Jackson sat in the car adjusting the mirrors and seat. Now who adjusts those *after* the car is parked? I'm thinking it wasn't Jackson, it was our killer. Then he put on Jackson's hat and sunglasses and exited the car, wearing Jackson's jacket. He walked into the woods in the direction of where we found the body, keeping his back to the cameras. He must have found a different way out because he doesn't show up again in any of the park feeds. Tells me he was familiar with this area."

"That's great, Mitch! We may have a visual of our killer. What can you tell about him from that?"

"Well, looks like we're dealing with a white male, brown hair, approximately 6-foot-tall, about 200 pounds. That's an inch taller and a little heavier than Jackson. That's it, never got a look at his face."

"It's a start. How about Jackson's phone? Anything there?"

"Yeah, the phone." Mitch repeated under his breath as he flipped pages. When he found what he was looking for, he continued. "GPS was turned off, but text messages reveal that he was out drinking with friends on Saturday night. A bar called the Main Place, on Alexander Street. I swung by there on my way back to the station. Bartender, name of Jimmie, spelled with an ie, said Jackson left by himself just before two in the morning.

That he had been drinking heavy and tossing money around same as usual. He ordered chicken wings and french fries about an hour before he left the bar. Jimmie didn't notice anything different, Jackson didn't seem to be depressed or suicidal. In fact, he overheard Jackson and a couple of his friends planning a fishing trip for next weekend. Bartender vouched for the fact that all his friends remained at the bar for another hour after closing. Said they were eating snacks and drinking coffee. No cameras in the parking lot. I called a couple of his friends to confirm the bartender's information and one of them added that he did notice Jackson's car was still there when he left the bar. He thought maybe Jackson had thought better about driving drunk and had called a cab. I checked his phone and he never used it after 10:22 pm Saturday evening."

"So his killer could have been waiting for him outside the bar. Maybe he met someone he knew that offered him a ride? Would he have accepted a ride from a stranger in his condition?"

"Could be. No sign of a struggle in the parking lot."

"So the car was left at the bar early Sunday morning 'til we see it being parked Sunday afternoon. No one saw it being picked up?"

"Nobody reported seeing anything. Bar opened at 4 pm and we know the car was at the park by then."

Emma turned to her board. "So our timeline starts at 1:50 am Sunday morning when Jackson left the bar, to 8:30 am Monday morning when his body is discovered. That's 30 hours we need to account for."

Stepping back, she looked at the board while expressing her thoughts out loud. "Where were you, Mr. Jackson? And when did you die? Doc said less than 24 hours before ten this morning, so sometime after ten on Sunday morning. So where were you during the 8 or so hours between the time you left the bar and bled out? How did you get into the woods after you were dead? Those are questions we don't have answers for. We know the car was parked at 2:45 Sunday afternoon. He was dead by then. Was his body sitting in the woods already?" She paused. "Mitch, turn the feed from the parking lot over to patrol. Ask them to run all the plates in the lot and interview the owners to see if anyone was in the area where we found the body. Maybe someone saw something suspicious."

Mitch was scribbling in his notebook. "Got it. Anything else?"

"I called the police in California, they're going to notify his family. They're also getting dental records and sending them to Doc MacGee as another way to confirm our ID. I have the warrant to search his house, we'll go there next."

"Okay, got it." Mitch checked his notes. "Let me get the video feed over to the patrol Sergeant, let Doc know what time Jackson ate at the bar and ask Jack to get a crew to meet us at Jackson's house. That should do it, give me half an hour."

"Excellent, that gives me enough time to pop down and get one of those hot dogs. I forgot to eat lunch, until I smelled yours, that is. Now I've got to have one! I'll meet you at the corner in thirty."

Emma just finished eating when Mitch pulled up with the car. She climbed into the passenger side and buckled up. Checking her notes, she put Jackson's address into the GPS. "Head East," she told Mitch, "I have Jackson's address as 85 Westminster Road, off East Avenue."

"That's not far from Peter's house. Hmmm. Sorry. None of my business."

"Just a coincidence but I'll keep my eyes open from now on. Mitch, about this morning, I just want to say that I understand your concern and I appreciate the information you discovered. I intend to be vigilant. I don't want to be a stupmitten."

They pulled up to Jackson's address, and saw a couple of Jack's guys from this morning waiting for them.

"That's weird, I thought they would still be at the park." Mitch commented as they pulled up to the curb and stepped out of the car.

Brett walked over to them. "I just got off the radio with Sergent Z. I heard him calling for a crew for Jackson's house and I told him we'd take it. Good timing - we just finished up at the park."

"Good," said Mitch, "glad you're here. Means I don't have to rehash what we have; your crew is up to speed. Where's Jack?"

"He got called to another scene. Two kids got into a fight before school, one's dead, others in the hospital fighting for his life. Jack took a fresh crew to that one and sent us to follow up here to collect whatever evidence we find. I also have the keys from the scene. Jack said to turn them over to you. Hoping they'll unlock these doors so we don't have to break in."

The three of them walked down the long sidewalk up to the front door together. The house was a small, brick ranch. It looked out of place surrounded by the much larger, older homes that had been remodeled to hold multiple apartment units. The contrast between the humble one story home and the grand three story houses with leaded glass and covered porches was striking. Emma observed that Mr. Jackson would have enjoyed very little privacy. His neighbors would have been witness to every coming and going. Bad for him, but it might be good for us.

Mitch inserted the door key, and pushed the door open. Brett handed out gloves and booties as they stepped inside.

After two hours of careful examination, they came up empty. Nothing appeared to be disturbed. The beds were made, everything was where it should be. There were dinner dishes sitting in the sink. Leftover food still sticking to the plates. Two empty chicken pot pie boxes were in the trash. Brett left the premises with the electronics to report back to Jack, leaving behind a small crew to collect the food samples and secure the property.

Emma and Mitch returned to their car.

"Mitch, have a couple officers interview the tenants whose windows allow them a view of Jackson's driveway. I want them to conduct the interviews tonight to see if anyone saw Jackson returning home on Sunday morning after he left the bar. Perhaps we can find out who brought him home, if he did come home."

"The house is clean so he wasn't killed there. We still don't know where he was killed."

"Yeah, chances are we'll come up empty, but we have to eliminate possibilities, it's as important as discovering probabilities.

"I'll gather the reports in the morning and meet you in your office. I'll even bring breakfast," Mitch offered, as he turned over the engine.

Emma stared out the window while they motored back to the station, absorbed in her thoughts. Peter's house was only a few blocks away from Jackson's. Odd she was in this neighborhood so often these last few days. She smiled a bit thinking of Peter and touched the medallion around her neck. She recalled the fantastic meal they enjoyed together at the restaurant and the gourmet lunch in his home. How could that be the same man Mitch told her about? Could she be so easily seduced by his money and allure?

"What're you thinking about?" Mitch asked her.

"Food. A body can't be thinking about murder all the time."

"Funny, that's what I was thinking about."

"Yeah! What are the odds!"

## CHAPTER 22

After her hectic day, Emma was looking forward to a quiet, stress free evening to immerse herself in her exercise routine. She could use the time to contemplate her diverse feelings regarding Mr. Peter Hartman. Her plan for a quick bite to eat was dashed when she opened her empty refrigerator and was reminded that she needed to go grocery shopping. For a moment she considered running down to Wegmans grocery store to grab a hot rotisserie chicken. Then she spotted an energy bar in the back of her cupboard and decided it would suffice. She made out a grocery list while she ate her protein bar. The list grew as she checked her cupboards and found she was out of most of the staples she enjoyed. She remembered eating the last of the peanut butter and crackers that morning for breakfast. She would have to go tomorrow for sure. She felt better when she put the completed list into her purse. Organization was the key to happiness her Aunt Maggie always said. Must have been true, she was one hundred and three when she departed this life.

Emma had just finished changing into her workout clothes when she heard a loud commotion outside her door.

"Emma, Emma! Are you in there? I have to talk to you, unlock the door! Hurry girl, it's important."

"What in the world?" Emma strode over to the door. "My Lord Jean, what's so important that you're trying to knock my door down?" She unlocked and opened the door, trying not to show her annoyance that her plans were being interrupted. The bundle of nervous energy that lived next door, flowed quickly through the open door.

"What took you so long? Never mind, I'm just glad you're home. Lock the door!"

"Slow down Jean, what in the world has you so riled up?"

"It's about Peter! Emma, he's a dangerous man!"

"You too Jean? You're checking him out, too?"

"Huh? No, nothing like that, what do you mean, too? Oh never mind, sit down and I'll explain. Lock the door first." Jean made a half hearted attempt to sit down at the kitchen counter to wait for Emma.

Emma closed and locked the door as Jean made frantic motions with her hands, as if to help speed the process along.

When Emma finished, she turned and looked at Jean, "I'd offer you something to eat, but my cupboard is bare. Would you like a drink, a soothing cup of tea perhaps?"

"No Emma, this is important! Now listen for a change damn it!" Jean was becoming more animated, sitting then standing and finally sitting again. She set both hands, palms down, on the countertop and paused long enough to inhale, trying to contain her emotions so what she had to say would be understood. Emma sat down across from her to listen.

"Okay girlfriend, you have my undivided attention, what's got you so upset?"

"I ran into my editor this morning when I handed in my column. We went out for breakfast and I was telling him about you and Peter. He said the name was familiar. He remembered something about a Peter Hartman from years ago. Anyway, he just called me and told me that he went back to the newspaper and searched the archives. He found several stories about Peter Hartman and Hartman Enterprises that referred to suspected links to criminal activities in the U.S. and in Europe. Did you know that Peter used to have a partner? Described as a charming Irishman named Ryan Kelly who was in charge of the European branch of Hartman Enterprises. He was murdered in London about six years ago. Police thought it was a suicide at first, but little things didn't add up. Scotland yard did a thorough investigation and connected it to a professional hit man that disguised his killings to look like accidents or suicides. No one was ever charged, then, a few days later, there was an attempt on Peter's life in New York City. He was in his hotel room when he was shot. New York City police suspected it was a professional hit and that Peter was just lucky he wasn't killed. But my editor thinks that luck had nothing to do with it. In his opinion, Peter was covering his tracks and Peter put out the hit on his own partner and a miss on himself. Peter became sole owner of Hartman Enterprises when Ryan Kelly died. That's when he changed the name to Peter Hartman Enterprises. That's a powerful motive if you ask me." Jean sat back and paused to take a breath.

Emma had listened to every word pouring out of her friend's mouth. She struggled to contain her emotions so her trained mind could evaluate this disturbing information. Combined with the particulars Mitch had given her that morning, she was beginning to get a clearer picture of Peter Hartman and things weren't looking good. Her hand went to the necklace that Peter had given her and she shivered. Without thinking, she unclipped it and removed it from around her neck. She stared at it as she held it in her hand. Overwhelming emotions boiled up from the pit of her stomach. Feelings of being deceived and violated by the same man who had given her that beautiful symbol of protection. Exasperation took over and she threw the necklace across the room as hard as she could. The medallion hit the brick surround on her gas fireplace with a loud thud and broke into several pieces that fell onto the metal floor insert, making tinkling sounds as they landed.

Jean gasped and jumped out of her chair. "Emma, what did you do? Oh my God, I didn't expect this reaction! I had to tell you! You had to know." She walked over to retrieve the broken necklace. As she picked up the pieces, she admonished Emma. "You broke it into a million pieces except for the chain. At least it's a nice gold chain, you can still use that. Wait a minute Em… what the hell...?" She paused to look at one piece in particular. What the hell is this?"

Emma walked over to where Jean was kneeling on the floor examining the small object. Emma reached out her hand and Jean dropped the tiny piece of metal into it.

"This looks like an RFID! That son of a bitch! All that sweet talk and the phony jerk was monitoring me! These damn things are getting smaller all the time."

"What the hell are you talking about Em? What is it?"

"A radio frequency identification chip. They were originally developed to locate missing pets, cars and other types of property. I didn't realize they had gotten this small and sophisticated. They use electromagnetic fields to transfer data wirelessly. I feel like such a fool Jean, me a successful detective with the RPD, I was sucked right in with all his charm like a lovesick teenager! Why would anyone do this? What's the point of tracking me? What did he expect to learn? Why now?" Emma walked over to her kitchen drawer and pulled out a Coddington magnifying glass to get a closer look.

"Could it have something to do with a case you're working on?" Jean asked. "You met Peter the same day you started working a new case."

"Yeah. That's true, but I don't see any connection. I guess it could have... oh, I don't know. And good as this magnifier is, it's not good enough. I'll need to take this to work and have EU take a look at it." Emma dug out a small baggie and deposited the bug into it and placed them in her purse. "Why would Peter pretend to have a romantic interest in me? Can I be fooled so easily by a little sweet talk over dinner? I don't understand the purpose of any of this. There has to be something I'm missing. There's a reason for everything. Why would he be stalking me? What does he expect to learn by keeping track of my movements?" Emma paced back and forth in the living room, turning and flipping the data over in her mind while she watched Jean finish picking up the pieces of the necklace then sit in silence waiting for her to say something.

"Unbelievable," was all Emma kept saying over and over. Tomorrow she would do a complete background check on Mr. Peter Hartman and his so called, cook/bodyguard, Mr. Gordon Kleinman. Peter had mentioned during their stroll at the Lilac Festival that he had a girlfriend who died. Did he tell her how she died? No, Emma didn't think so. She would have to check that out too. And she would have to keep the chip with her so he wouldn't suspect that she had found it. The thought of allowing him to continue monitoring her made her stomach turn. She felt so violated, he had played her and she fell for it like a naive teenager. She stopped pacing and sat down across from Jean.

"Who does he think he's messing with, I'll throw the book at him. He'll get no mercy from me!"

"Emma, I'm so sorry it worked out this way."

"Not your fault. I was such a fool! I can imagine what Mitch's reaction will be when I tell him."

"Do you have to tell him?"

"Trust me, if there was any way to leave him out of this, I would. No, I have to tell him. He'd better not gloat or give me that, "told you so" look."

"He wouldn't do that."

"You're right, Mitch always reacts in a professional manner. That's one thing that I can count on. I wonder if I'm more upset that I've been played for a fool, or that Mitch was right. The only thing I know for sure is I am beyond angry!"

"Em, why don't you start on the punching bag and I'll ride the bike. We can work out together tonight."

"Great idea Jean, thanks for keeping me company."

Emma walked over to the bench and grabbed her gloves. She needed to punch something and couldn't wait to get at that punching bag. Tonight it had a name and that name was Peter!

## CHAPTER 23

Alexander was well rested after a day of quiet reflection regarding the direction his life was taking. He had spent the day attending to routine tasks. A trip to the barber shop for a relaxing shave and a haircut, bill paying and grocery shopping. He spent the evening writing in his journal. He experienced an unpleasant surprise yesterday afternoon when he accessed a website that reported local news. It reported the circumstances of a couple finding Jackson's body that morning in the woods. It announced that the police were investigating the death. He was disturbed when he first heard the revelation. He had not expected the body to be found so soon. He thought it would be several days, even weeks if he was lucky, before they stumbled across the body. The more time elapsed he knew, the more difficult it would be for them to determine the exact time of death but he was still safe. They would not be able to figure out what had happened. He was convinced that he had prepared well and resolved not to allow his mood to be brought down because they had found the body sooner than he had planned. The reporter stated that Jackson had died from what appeared to be a self-inflicted wound to the leg. Alexander chuckled with pride. The national television media soon picked up the story and used their on-air time to continue to discuss and summarize the details of Jackson's murder trial and how the prosecution had failed to bring him to justice for the murder of his wife. The news was all about his wife's murder, not his. How ironic! Alexander was pleased with the unforeseen direction the media was taking the story. He was not pleased, however, to learn that Detective Emma Mason had been called to the scene, even though he was confident she wouldn't connect the two deaths. Regardless, he was determined not to let anything spoil his day of celebration. He was on top of the world and oblivious to what a long fall it might be if he were to come tumbling down.

Today he would begin his next adventure. Alexander smiled as he imagined killing his next target. This one was personal; this was the man who took the lives of his beloved parents. He would now prepare for the elimination of the man who had committed those horrendous murders right here in this very house. At first he had thought he should wait to get more experience in killing, but he felt ready. He didn't see the advantage of waiting, and besides he simply didn't want to.

Alexander was looking forward to facing Jethro Mercier one last time. He assured himself that he had honed his skills enough with the successful eliminations of Luther Maxwell and Edward Jackson, and was confident in his ability to continue his mission without the police ever connecting him to the murders. Alexander was very proud of the skillful and knowledgeable methods he had employed to execute his targets and how he had been able to conceal his involvement, but to be fair, it turned out the police were easy to deceive.

Alexander typed the man's name into his search engine... the name he hated above all others... the name of the repulsive, loathsome monster that had murdered his parents. Jethro Mercier. An ironic twist, he reflected, to carry the name Mercier when he had showed none to his victims. Well, the tables were about to turn. Alexander smiled as he imagined swinging the bat and smashing Jethro's head in. But only after he had caused him to suffer by breaking every major bone in his body. Oh, he would take intense pleasure in watching this man die a slow and very painful death. Perhaps he should research the word "torture". Mankind has devised numerous ways of inflicting severe pain on one another over the centuries. He wondered if there were any other animals that spent time inventing new ways to torture others of their own species? Was mankind the only one capable of feeling pleasure when watching another suffer pain? Were human beings the only ones to elevate torture to an art form? Yes, he still had much to learn on the wonderful world wide web.

So far he had been able to cover his involvement by making the murders appear to be suicides, an idea he had heard about in Peter's house. Alexander knew that beating Jethro with a bat could never be made to look like a suicide. He chuckled at the thought of the man trying to beat himself to death, recalling scenes from Fight Club. In his mind, however, there was no other way for Jethro to die but by the method he employed to murder his parents. After much thought, it occurred to him that if he destroyed the man's body to the point that identification would be impossible, there would be no reason for the police to list himself as a person of interest. Jethro Mercier would just cease to exist and only he and Jethro would know the truth. The all-important how and why he left this earth. The only downside to that plan, was that Alexander would have to abandon his fantasy of Emma Mason coming to tell him that the man who had killed his parents was dead. He had daydreamed of how he would react when she delivered the news. His imagination had filled many hours with pleasurable thoughts of how he would react to Emma's words. Alas, as the saying goes, you can't have your cake and eat it too. The reality was that he could not have it both ways, the choice was obvious. He would enjoy eliminating the man more. Erasing his pathetic existence off the planet forever. No one would miss him, no one would report him missing. Alexander would remove any way of identifying the man so he would just disappear into oblivion, allowing Alexander to go on uninterrupted, continuing his important mission of helping the police protect and serve the public.

He thought about how he would savor every minute of tracking and eliminating his prey, however long it took. He was a patient man and was enjoying the anticipation as he imagined the pleasure he would experience when he heard Jethro struggling for his last breath as he died.

For now, he needed to research everything... find out his likes and dislikes. Check out the social media sites, all the public and private sites that sold information. Alexander continued to be amazed at the amount of information available to the public with just a few keystrokes. How much he could learn about a person while he sat at his desk. Comfortable and secure, in his own home surfing the web! This should be against the law, he thought as he sipped his cup of tea and nibbled on caviar and crackers. Ah, he sighed, this was how life was meant to be enjoyed by people of superior intellect like himself.

His computer searches soon revealed that Jethro was not employed anywhere, however, he did sometimes work for an independent caterer making deliveries for tips. Other than that, he had no visible means of support. He lived with a grandmother off and on when he was not shacked up with one of his various lady friends. Alexander considered his options with great care. The fact that Jethro knew who he was and what he looked like would be a huge disadvantage. It had only been a year since they had seen each other on a daily basis at Jethro's trial, so Alexander would not be able to approach him in person. If he ordered food to be delivered, he couldn't use his own address, Jethro knew the house and wouldn't come to the front door, virtually delivering himself to die. Alexander was amused by the thought. Besides, there was no way to ensure that Jethro would be assigned to make the delivery.

Alexander had to consider Jethro's size and strength. Physically they were the same size, but Jethro was younger, so wrestling him into submission was not a plausible option. This was a kid that grew up on the streets so he would be alert and cautious of suspicious people lurking about. This was going to be more difficult than the others, but the reward would be worth all the extra effort.

Alexander was confident he would figure it out in due time. He would think of an acceptable plan that would be infallible. He wondered if Jethro could feel that his days were numbered? A premonition, perhaps, that he would soon pay, in kind, for his terrible deeds.

Alexander just had to devise a way to get Jethro alone, in an isolated place, where he could take his time beating him to death like Jethro had done to his parents. He had to think of a flawless plan, one that would serve his needs while diminishing the chance the police would suspect him in case they were able to find and identify the body. This would take considerable planning but Alexander was obsessed at this point. He began to work out scenarios and strategies. Each time he would find major flaws and would have to abandon the plan and start over. He worked late into the night, reading and rereading all the information he had accumulated, looking for Jethro's Achilles heel.

Money seemed to be the major motivator in Jethro's life, or more to the point, the lack of money. There had to be a way to use that fact to his advantage. Alexander wondered if he could pretend he wanted to hire him, but why? To beat someone? That might work, but how could he approach him? He couldn't do it on the computer, too easy to trace, besides, in all likelihood, he wouldn't fall for that anyway, if he even had access to one. No, that was another dead end.

He had to find someone to work through, someone that Jethro trusted, but how? Who? Wait - what about the dubious ladies he spent time with? Without doubt they would need money as much as Jethro. Perhaps he could hire one of them to... to what? He needed to figure out a plan and work through one of them, but which one? And how? He started typing again. Now he needed to research the women in Jethro's life. Look for a weak link, someone with a low I.Q and even lower self-esteem. A person who Alexander could easily manipulate so they would be unaware of the fact that they were complicit in Jethro's death.

After an hour of visiting most of the available social sites on the internet, Alexander found the Facebook page of a lady of questionable repute by the name of Ginny Peckallo. She too, had no visible means of support and appeared to be willing to do most anything for money. Alexander had sometimes seen her in photos with Jethro posted on his Facebook page. They were usually shown in compromising positions indicating an intimate relationship of some type. He discovered that her Facebook page had been updated three days earlier to indicate that she was now in a relationship with Jethro Mercier. Further investigation divulged that Jethro had been living with her for the last few days. Her own page was wide open to anyone who cared to look and she was careful to include the fact that she was still available for part-time employment to any of her past clients.

Feeling quite smug, he scrolled through the numerous trashy photos she posted. Some of which came dangerously close to violating Facebook's content policies. How can people be so oblivious to the fact that the messages and photos they're posting will travel all over the world? After thinking about it, he realized she had to be aware she was providing entertainment for those with repugnant thoughts. She was, no doubt, an exhibitionist at her core. Regardless, she was a contemptible piece of work. He chuckled, as he took time to study each one of her photos in detail. Thank God for women with self-esteem issues.

In time, even Ginny's dicey escapades failed to hold his attention as his eyelids fought to stay open while his brain had already begun the process of shutting down for the night. With reluctance, he logged off his computer. Alexander was ready for sleep. His plan was formulated and tomorrow he would begin the hunt renewed and refreshed. He had formulated a killer plan.

## CHAPTER 24

Emma was sitting at her desk, filled with apprehension as she waited for Mitch. She looked down at her desk when he walked into her office with the reports, two bags of food and two steaming cups of coffee which he set on her desk with great ceremony.

"Good morning, sunshine! I have brought you breakfast sandwiches with sides of potatoes and jelly filled donuts for dessert. A nutritious breakfast, as promised."

"Thanks Mitch, have a seat."

Mitch's chatter came to an abrupt halt when Emma raised her head and looked into his eyes. "You don't look so good, Em, what's wrong?"

"It's Peter and I don't know where to start, except to say you were right. Turns out, I was a big stupmitten."

"Whoa, hold on a minute, that's not like you Em!" Mitch walked around the desk and stood behind Emma, placing his hands on her shoulders and began to massage them. "Tell me what happened and we'll figure out what to do. No matter what happened, you're a survivor, Emma."

Emma sat in stunned silence. This was the first time Mitch had ever touched her in this manner and it felt very strange. She had expected him to gloat. Get angry perhaps. But what she didn't expect was this show of sympathy and concern. Not like this. Not from Mitch. He was always, to her way of thinking, a disciplined Marine. This was so unexpected after her restless night of self-examination, she felt herself close to tears. "Stop it

Mitch! What the hell do you think you're doing?" she snapped at him.

Mitch flinched at her words. "Sorry, you just looked so defeated, like a pathetic loser sitting there licking your wounds. Almost like you forgot you're a cop."

Emma understood his words were meant to help them both get back on track and she was grateful. She took a deep breath as Mitch circled back around to the front of her desk and sat down.

"So spill Detective, what happened last night?"

"Jean came over. She said her editor had recognized Peter's name and when he checked the newspaper archives he found additional information. I combined that with what you told me yesterday and it appears Mr. Peter Hartman is a deceitful, untrustworthy criminal. Purhaps even a murderer."

"That bad? I'm really sorry Em."

While they ate their breakfast Emma gave him all the particulars then showed him the bug that had been hidden in her medallion. Once again they had drawn the curtain between their professional and personal lives and were examining the facts of the situation like seasoned police officers searching for answers.

Mitch's pencil was flying over his notebook as he attempted to keep up with Emma's rapid recital of information. He summarized, "so today I'll do a complete background check on Peter Hartman, Ryan Kelly and on Peter Hartman Enterprises."

"While you're at it Mitch, check the background of his so-called cook, Gordon Kleinman, and his wife, I think they may have come from Germany. Come to think of it, I'd like to know more about the girlfriend that died last year. Who was she and how did she die?"

"Do you have a first name for Gordon's wife or any information on the girlfriend?"

"No, I never asked. Do me another favor, would you? Take this bug and have our technical unit see what information it was broadcasting and where the information was going. Can they do that?"

"Yeah, it might take a day or two, but I'm sure they can get that information. Meanwhile, I'll see if they can disable it in a way that won't arouse suspicion."

"That would be great if they can do that, otherwise I'll just continue to carry it around with me so we won't tip him off that it's been discovered."

"I don't understand the point of tracking you like that. He was taking a big risk if he got caught."

"You'd think so, but I checked this morning to see what I could charge him with. I was disappointed to learn that the law hasn't caught up with this technology. The closest I can get is a class B misdemeanor for unlawful possession or use of a radio device. I gotta tell you, any fine he may have to pay won't soothe my outrage. Being tracked like an animal! I can't believe how violated and pissed off I feel. I want to put him in jail and then…"

Emma's tirade was interrupted by a knock on her door. She looked up to see a smiling officer Geraci grinning at her from the other side of the glass insert. Mitch moved to the door and opened it.

"Come in, officer. What have you got?"

Mitch began consuming his second serving of hash browned potatoes as Geraci entered the room. The young officer was quivering with excitement, obviously proud of whatever he had uncovered.

"I went to the Brick and Nail after work yesterday and our witness, Rose Marie was just finishing her shift. We went to a little coffee shop nearby to discuss the case. She told me that she remembered Maxwell had mentioned "Lincoln". I asked her if that was the name of Maxwell's new friend. She said no, it was the name of the friend's car. She didn't pay attention to the man's name, just the model of his car. I asked her to call me if she remembers anything else."

"Good work, officer. That information could be helpful if we find a suspect. I commend you for going the extra mile in the pursuit of justice. Hope it wasn't too much trouble for you."

"Yes ma'am, I mean no ma'am. I want you to know I'm planning on continuing the interview with our witness this weekend, over lunch. That is unless you have an objection."

"None at all, Miss Pacelli is not a suspect in this case, you can continue to date her officer."

"Good to know, thank you." Officer Geraci was smiling happily as he turned and slipped out the door, closing it behind him.

"I really like Geraci, he's got good instincts and a sense of humor. If he doesn't screw up, he could go a long way in this department. What do you think Mitch?"

"Yeah, it appears he's dedicated to the job, and he thinks like a cop. That's always a good sign. So, now we know our guy drives a Lincoln. We can add that to the board."

"How about Doc and Jack? Have we heard from either of them today?"

Mitch opened his notebook and flipped through the pages. "Doc said he'd have his report ready for us this morning, but off the record, told me he thinks T.O.D. was earlier than he first thought. No word from Jack."

"Anything else?"

"Yeah, couple of things. Checked Jackson's car for fingerprints, fibers, dirt in the tires, any trace evidence. Car was clean. We knew the driver was wearing gloves, but I hoped we'd find something, but nada. Patrol conducted interviews with the owners of the cars parked in the lot on Sunday. Officer Carris gave me an oral update this morning and said none of them observed anything that would help. We'll get the complete report later today or tomorrow."

"As we both know; the absence of evidence can often be just as important. I'll bet Jackson's body was placed there late Sunday night or early Monday morning. What else have you got?"

"That's it, until we talk with Doc."

"Great. You get started on Peter's background while I add these new facts to the board, run a few scenarios and see what I come up with. By the way, the computer generated a 68% chance that our two victims are connected, so that was an excellent catch, Mitch. Good work."

Mitch slipped his notebook into his pocket and dug into the bag of donuts still sitting on the desk. Mitch took out the two donuts, leaving one on a napkin in front of Emma, and put the other in his mouth. Emma watched him take a big bite, before he scooped up all the trash from their morning meal and headed for the door. He stopped to look at her. "Live in the moment Em, eat the donut. You deserve it! It's mmm mmm good!"

Emma smiled as Mitch walked out and closed the door. She thought about telling him not to talk with food in his mouth, but thought better of it. Seemed to her, Mitch was seldom without food in his mouth. She felt relieved that he was on board and felt a warm, comfortable emotion stirring inside. It must be the donut, she decided as she gave in to temptation and picked it up to examine it. She lifted it first to her nose, to inhale the sweet smell of the pastry, then with great anticipation, she took a small bite, savoring the flavors of jam, icing and fried dough melting in her mouth. She took her time, chewing that first bite with her eyes closed so she could concentrate on the flavors she so often denied herself. Perhaps this was what heaven would be like. All her senses concentrated on one delightful experience. Mmm

mmm good. Mitch was right! There is much to be said about living in the moment, especially when that particular moment involves a jelly filled, fried donut with thick icing layered on top.

It was late morning when Mitch and Emma made their way down to Doc's office located across the hall from the morgue. Doc MacGee was typing on his computer, working on one of the numerous reports lined up on his desk. He glanced up when the door opened and nodded, "Good timing, just finishing the Jackson report. Make yourselves comfortable, I'll be just a minute longer."

Emma and Mitch walked in and sat down in the two soft, overstuffed chairs closest to Doc's desk. Emma knew that Mitch would be eyeballing the couch preferring a quick nap while they waited. She wondered if Doc took power naps at work. Couldn't blame if he did, with all the responsibilities he had as County Coroner. She knew Doc's job included discussing with families the circumstances surrounding the deaths of their loved one. Because of that, his office was decorated in soothing neutrals with soft lighting and cozy furniture. An abundance of natural objects such as geodes, bones, shells, and fossils were scattered throughout. One entire wall consisted of bookshelves chock full of numerous titles interspersed with these myriad objects - in and of itself a work of art. Many of the books were Doc's medical reference books, but other titles dealt with assisting survivors cope with their loss. These were in multiples, suitable for different ages, intended to be loaned out to survivors to help them deal with the raw emotions associated with the sudden and unexpected loss of a loved one. Few of those extra copies ever came back, but if and when they did, Doc used the opportunity to offer additional advice and counsel to the bereaved. He was a unique and sensitive man, devoted to the study of the fundamental nature of our existence and possessed of uncanny wisdom, but also revered for his gallows humor among those who knew him well. Emma appreciated the many and varied contributions he made as part of their team.

Doc MacGee hit the Print button on his computer, and collected the report as it exited the printer. He handed the pages to Emma.

"This Jackson case had me stumped. I had two different times of death from his body, which, as we know, is impossible. I had to do some detective work of my own. It's all in my report, but here's the gist of it. I took the liver temp at the scene, that indicated he'd been dead for between 18 and 24 hours. This morning, Mitch gave me the time he ate his chicken wings

Saturday evening. Yesterday Brett brought me remnants of the chicken pot pie found on the dishes in his home. I pinpointed the age of the pot pie based on decomposition at known room temperature and compared that to the stomach contents and the known rate of digestion. I did the same for the wings and fries he ate at the bar. Both foods confirm that Jackson died two or three hours after eating his last meal, which would have been 31 to 33 hours before I examined the body. Now I have to account for my original erroneous calculation and that is where my entomologist comes in. Ted took samples of the ground under and around the body, and using the known rate of decay, he was able to determine the approximate length of time the blood was in the ground. His tests confirm that the blood entered the ground between 3 and 4 o'clock Monday morning, long after Jackson was dead. So in conclusion, I have determined that Mr. Jackson must have died between 2:30 am and 3:30 am Sunday morning, his body was kept in a cold environment of some kind in an attempt to disguise the TOD. It was then placed in the woods where our killer poured the victim's blood into the ground, under the wound, in an attempt to make it appear that he had died at the scene of an apparent suicide."

"Excellent work Doc! That TOD lines up with the reports Mitch has from visitors to the park on Sunday. No one saw or heard anything that would lead us to believe the body was in the woods on that day." Emma said.

Doc nodded his agreement. "A pretty elaborate scenario considering all the effort and planning that was needed to pull it off."

"It would have worked too, if Mitch hadn't noticed the clean shoes, which in turn caused us to question everything else we discovered at the scene. Such a little thing, but it's always the little things that help us catch the killers. Now that we know it was staged we can study how it was done, and hope that will help us uncover a suspect. Great job, both of you." Emma nodded her approval.

"Yeah, thanks Doc," Mitch added, "this report will be a great help. By the way, Emma tells me you and your wife are expecting your first grandchild. Congratulations! My mother has two from my sister and her husband. Mom claims that grandchildren are the reward God gives you for not killing your kids when they're teenagers!"

Doc laughed out loud. "That's funny Mitch! Probably because there's so much truth to it! Jennie is our oldest and there were times we were at our wits end, trying to set limits without it turning into all out warfare. Even after she left home for college, we felt compelled to warn her at every opportunity about the danger around every corner. Somehow she survived our futile attempts to control her life and she turned out just fine." He chuckled, "Okay, that's enough, I have a backlog of bodies waiting for me, I trust you can see yourselves out."

Emma and Mitch climbed the stairs in a determined manner that somehow morphed into an unspoken challenge of attempting to best each other to the top. Once they reached their floor, Mitch grabbed the door and opened it with a flourish. Neither of them acknowledged that they were racing or that Mitch had won. Emma paused to catch her breath. "I have just enough time before lunch to update my timeline and combine this new information in my computer. I'll run some stats, see what we've got. I'll meet with Jack after lunch. Catch up with you later today. We have a few more loose ends to tie up, let's hope they lead to a suspect before we have another victim to add to the growing list. By the way, thanks for the donut, it was beyond delish."

"Before you go, Emma, I have more information for you. Peter's girlfriend's name was Susan LaMonte, and she died of a very aggressive form of breast cancer at age 32. Doctor I spoke with said he had recommended a complete mastectomy. He thought it would have given her a better chance than just the chemo. Susan chose to take her chances, said she was too young to lose her breasts. Doctor said she passed away three months after she was diagnosed. The Doc added that Peter urged Susan to get the mastectomy but in the end, he supported the fact that it was her decision. He also said that he thought Peter was devoted to Susan and he stayed by her side to the end. He also paid all her medical bills."

"Thanks Mitch, good to know I wasn't completely wrong about the guy. That's such a sad story though. Makes me wonder what I would do faced with that kind of decision. I think I would do whatever gave me the best chance to survive, but you never know. So easy to look at it in the abstract. I hope that I never have to face that decision."

"True enough! Maybe that's why men refuse to see doctors on a regular basis, we don't want to have to make those life or death decisions."

"Oh, you would rather find out when it's too late. When you have no choice but to die?"

"Well, it sounds dumb when you put it that way, but the way that I see it, our choice of career puts us into enough danger without having to fight a life threatening disease. Anyway, I'll get on Hartman's background next. Don't forget to eat lunch!" Mitch turned and made his way down the hallway to his office with renewed energy.

She might have been imagining it, but Emma thought she saw him do a little sideways kick. She wondered at what age a man could be considered grown up? Truth was, she didn't know if many of them even had the desire to complete the process. Maybe they had the right idea, never give up your inner child. She turned and skipped down the empty hallway to her office.

## CHAPTER 25

Emma phoned Jack to make sure he was in before she climbed the stairs to see him. His report was ready, as usual. She spotted a new picture on his desk. It was of Jack, his wife, two boys and two large, playful looking dogs sitting at their feet.

"So, this the new dog you decided to adopt?" Emma lifted the picture off his desk and made a show of examining it. "Looks like he's made himself right at home."

"Herself, and yeah, I admit, it was love at first sight. I told Anne, no more, but I really like this little lady, she completes our family. Nothing like being greeted by two excited dogs every time you walk in the door. They give me balance from all the carnage we have to deal with. You should think about getting a dog yourself, Emma."

"No that's okay, I have no room for a dog in my life right now, besides I have my neighbor, Jean keeps me grounded and company when I want it. Plus, I don't have to take her out for a walk every day. You find anything at the scene that will help us?"

"We examined the ground for footprints and found places where they had been brushed away. We followed the trail back to the railroad tracks and then lost it. But noted that we didn't find any of Jackson's footprints either. Ted verified there was no dirt from the area on Jackson's shoes. Traced the knife using a serial number we found on it. It belonged to Jackson. The car was clean, nothing there. Brett didn't find anything at the house or in the electronics to give us a lead on a suspect. I'm afraid we hit a dead end. Other than proving it was murder, not suicide. This time looks like our killer may have gotten away clean. I'm wondering if he doesn't have training of some kind in forensics or crime scene evaluation. It's all in my report."

Emma pulled some papers out of the file she had carried in with her. "Patrol interviewed Jackson's neighbors, they verified that Jackson never came home after he left Saturday evening. One of his neighbors said she had a fight with her husband and was up till 3 am watching TV. Her window faces Jackson's driveway; she would have seen the headlights or heard the garage door open if he had come home. We know he died within an hour or two of leaving the bar, so it's a safe assumption that he walked out of his house Saturday evening and never returned."

"Well, I know our job is to catch the bad guys, but as far as I'm concerned, Jackson was a wife killer who was able to buy his way out of prison and got away with murder. We have nothing to go on, why not let this one go cold?"

Emma stood up to leave, "I know, sometimes it's hard to tell the good from the bad but you know as well as I that our job is to gather evidence and determine what happened to the best of our abilities. The D.A. determines whether to bring charges, juries determine guilt and judges determine punishment. That's how our system works, when we blur the lines, justice will fail."

"True enough Detective, but sometimes justice fails in spite of our best efforts. Sometimes justice gets all tangled up in the grey areas and the guilty go free."

"We can't let ourselves get discouraged Jack."

"I know. Ninety nine percent of the time I'm good with that. Later detective."

Emma returned to her office where she spent the afternoon staying busy working on her computer, combining the two crimes, looking for possibilities and searching for loose ends that might reveal an area worth investigating once they were merged.

When Mitch stepped into her office she was engrossed in trying to connect the pieces of the puzzle. Mitch looked at the half eaten sandwich on her desk, sitting next to the cup of cold coffee from that morning.

"I see you're paying close attention to your nutritional needs again."

"Stop. I wasn't hungry. Besides, Jean and I are going to a buffet tonight and I want to be hungry so I can get my money's worth. What have you got?"

"I was able to get some background on the Kleinman's.

They were both born and raised in Germany. Her first name is Vera. They were trained Waffen-SS which is the German Armed Protection Squad. They met and married while they were both in service. After they left the military, they moved to Ireland where Gordon was hired by Ryan Kelly as his bodyguard. Over the years Ryan and Gordon became close friends. Peter hired them as his 'cook and housekeeper' after Kelly was murdered and they have been with him ever since. In fact, Peter bought the house on East Avenue after he hired them and the Kleinman's live with him in a separate apartment in the back of his house."

"Did Peter have a bodyguard before he hired the Kleinman's?"

"It doesn't look like it. He hired the Kleinman's after his partner was murdered and the attempt was made on his life. Oh, and here's the bug you found." Mitch set it on her desk. "The e-geeks took all the information they needed to trace it, but you'll have to keep it with you when you go home so he doesn't get suspicious. They said it's only a positioning device. It transmits your position so he can keep track of where you are, that's all."

"ONLY! That's enough! It's so creepy knowing that your every move is being monitored. Thanks Mitch, I'll just throw it in my purse until we find out what he hopes to learn with it. See you tomorrow and thanks for, well, for helping and understanding."

"You're welcome, enjoy your dinner with Jean and stay safe, Emma."

Emma left work and drove to the grocery store. She took a winding, zigzag path, picturing Peter watching and wondering where she was going and what she was going to do there. The thought crossed her mind to include a casual drive past his house. That would fry his bacon. She was amused by the thought, but the reality of the situation was that the bug in her purse gave her intense feelings of disdain and repulsion. Glancing at the clock on her dashboard, she realized she had wasted too much time.

She had to meet Jean soon. She drove to her local Wegmans store to pick up the items on her list. She walked through the store at a brisk pace, putting items into her cart and checking them off her list. When she approached the frozen foods, she found herself drawn to the ice cream case. Without hesitation, she reached in and pulled out a container of Death by Chocolate and dropped it into her cart. Then she backtracked to acquire a can of whipped cream and a banana. Might as well go whole hog, I'm off my diet anyway after that donut. I eat an ounce of ice cream and gain a pound of fat, but who cares. Might just as well jump in with both feet if you're going to jump. Diet be damned tonight, she decided. She would invite Jean to her house for dessert after dinner. They had a lot to discuss and there was no better way to clear your thoughts than a big bowl of ice cream sitting on top of fresh sliced bananas, piled high with whipped cream and topped with peanuts and a cherry. That should clear out the cobwebs in her mind. If only to add room for more fat cells.

CHAPTER 26

The next day Mitch walked into her office eating his breakfast.

"That's really disturbing Mitch, I don't understand how you can eat a banana smashed between two glazed donuts and call it breakfast!"

"Well what would you call it?"

"Disgusting, repugnant, appalling all come to mind."

"Don't knock it 'til you've tried it."

"Thanks but no thanks, I'll pass. Let's check out the timelines we have so far. We know when Jackson died, but we don't know where, or where his body was stored until it was dumped in the woods sometime early Monday morning. Could have been the same place. According to Doc's report, we know the body was refrigerated somehow."

"How about we look at the differences and similarities?"

"Okay, Jackson, no crime scene. Maxwell, we have the crime scene, he was killed and died where we found his body. Two different methods were used, one was a gun, the other was a knife. One body was moved, the other wasn't. The similarities; both were killed using their own weapon, both robbed of their cash, both made to look like suicide..." her voice trailed off.

"I don't see how we'll be able to find answers Emma, we're out of clues. We're also assuming that whoever committed these killings has nothing to do with the victims other than he killed them. Motive could be that we have a vigilante that is killing them because they got away with murder. I think using different weapons is because they were the weapon of choice when each of the victims committed their own crimes."

"It could just be convenience; those were the only weapons available at the time."

"I think it's more symbolic, Maxwell killed with a gun, Jackson killed with a knife. Live by the sword, die by the sword."

"You're quoting the Bible now! You think we're looking for a killer who's getting messages from God?"

"It's a possibility, wouldn't be the first killer who thought God was granting him divine guidance."

"Hmm, you could be right Mitch, it could be as simple as that. If that's the case, we may have to stand on the sidelines while the bodies pile up and we wait for our killer to make a mistake." Emma pictured bodies being stacked in a haphazard fashion all over the morgue with Doc MacGee eating his meals over them as he worked around the clock. "I'll defer to old fashioned police work instead. Let's go back and look into those original killings, maybe it's personal, someone's getting revenge against these particular men. Luther Maxwell, killed two people. Find out where Colleen Mark's fiancé is now, and any of her male relatives. Check all the males that match our killer's physical description. We can check to see if any of them drive a Lincoln."

"But that could have been rented so we can't use that to eliminate anyone."

"Good point Mitch. Jackson's wife had a father and a brother who have publicly stated their feelings. See if they've been in Rochester these last two weeks. I'll check out Maxwell's first murder, George Tyler, he had two brothers here in the city, see if anyone in his family is looking for revenge. Let's see if we can find anything new."

It was early afternoon when Emma was interrupted by a knock on her open door. She looked up to see Brigham holding flowers and grinning at her. She motioned for him to come in and watched while he set the flowers on her desk.

"Thanks, Brig but you really don't need to deliver these, just call me and I'll pick them up when I have time."

"Yes ma'am, but I don't mind. Enjoy the rest of your day, Detective Mason."

Emma waited for him to close the door and then looked for the card. It read: **All work and no play.**

**Call me to make a play date!! Peter.**

She took a deep breath, and then another. She knew that she had to confront him, but she still had not figured out why he was doing this, or what he was trying to accomplish with the bug, or if he was somehow connected to the two murders she was trying to solve. She placed a call to his answering service and was told he was busy but she could leave a message. "Just tell him that Emma Mason called, please".

"Oh, Miss Mason, please hold for one minute and I'll connect you."

A minute later Peter was on the phone. "Emma, it's so good to hear from you."

"I just got your flowers and I wanted to thank you in person. Will you be home this afternoon?"

"I have business to take care of, but I could be home by 5:30 if you want to come by. I'll have Gordon prepare dinner for us. It will be wonderful to see you again. There's something I need to discuss with you."

"Oh, that's interesting because I also have something I need to speak with you about. I'll see you around 6 then."

"It's a date. Looking forward to it, Emma. Good-bye for now."

Emma pushed the button with her finger and lifted it again for a new dial tone. She called Mitch and told him about the flowers and her plan to confront Peter at his house that evening.

"Hold on Emma, I have more information to give you, I'll be right there."

Five minutes later, Mitch was in her office. Emma noted that he wasn't eating anything, his entire manner was incisive and controlled, like a snake, coiled and ready to strike.

"Emma, I contacted a friend in the FBI and asked him to tell me whatever he could about the attempt on Hartman in New York City. He called me back this afternoon and told me that the bureau has been investigating Peter Hartman Enterprises off and on for the past six years. Some of this coincides with what Jean told you. It started six years ago. Scotland yard, along with the Belfast Harbour Police suspected that Ryan Kelly was using the company to run illegal guns into Ireland. Before they were prepared to make an arrest, Kelly's body was found in a London Hotel in what looked like a suicide. Next day, the Belfast Harbour Police got an anonymous tip and raided the Hartman warehouse in Ireland. They found crates full of illegal guns and ammunition. They confiscated everything, arrested the management of the warehouse and a couple of low level criminals but that is where it ended. They never uncovered the Mastermind of the operation. Meanwhile, Scotland yard matched Kelly's death to a professional hit man known as Accidental Al because he made his kills appear to be accidents or suicides. They traced Al to New York City where they discovered his body had been found tied to an abandoned pier at the waterfront. He was also suspected of the unsuccessful attempt to kill Peter Hartman. They have not been able to link Peter to the smuggling operation or the killings. For the past five years they have conducted sporadic searches and investigations and they are still waiting for him to slip up. My friend said that they would be most grateful for any help we can give them to bring Peter Hartman to justice."

"Sounds like he is very good at protecting himself while getting rich participating in illegal activities using his company as a cover."

"He hasn't escaped the law by being stupid or careless Em. You aren't going to just march in there and get a confession, remember Gordon and his wife are trained to protect Peter including killing anyone who threatens him."

"I know, I know. How about this. We'll bring in the FBI. I get wired and you and Geraci set up surveillance in a van outside Peter's house. I'll wear an earbud so you can talk to me and you can use the infrared thermal imaging camera to monitor the whereabouts of everyone in the house. If I get into trouble, you will be right there. Have one patrol car in the vicinity just in case."

"I don't know Emma, how about we just bring him in and question him where you aren't risking your life."

"You know as well as I do that we have zero evidence against him. The FBI has been working on him for six years. Maybe if I confront him, I'll catch him off guard and he'll slip up. It's worth a try Mitch. It's kind of weird, I know he's a dangerous man, but I also don't think he'll hurt me."

"That doesn't make any sense Emma. We know he's a criminal and he could be a killer. You're risking your life doing this, don't go in there with your guard down, that could be a fatal mistake."

"You're right, I have to talk to the Captain and get his approval for this operation and then get wired. Should be easy with the FBI's support. You get everything ready and set up in the van as soon as you can, so you're in place before Peter gets home at 5:30. I'll get there at 6, let's hope we get something useful out of this."

"Emma, you have to take time to eat, you're not at your best when you get run down. I'm going to call the deli and have them send up some food. What would you like?"

"Fine, how about a tuna melt with cheese. Tuna is supposed to be brain food. That should be good enough."

"Stay here until you've eaten, I'm getting you a chocolate milkshake to go with your sandwich, then you can prepare to do battle with the CEO of Peter Hartman Enterprises. Good luck, I got your back. Remember to keep your guard up, Emma, they play for keeps."

"Got it, eat and keep my guard up, but Mitch, I don't need the chocolate milkshake. I mean it."

"Okay, fine, how about a protein shake instead, you can always use more protein."

"Just get a move on, I'm calling the Captain's assistant to put me on his schedule as soon as she can. I need to talk to him face to face.

## CHAPTER 27

Alexander walked into the coffee shop closest to Ginny's address just before 10 am Wednesday. He had already purchased a used laptop from a pawn shop and had opened a new Facebook profile page under a fake name so he could contact her. He had considered many pseudonyms before deciding to adopt the name

Tony Stark, the name of the original avenger from the Avengers Comic book series. Alexander thought it most apropos. He ordered a coffee and breakfast sandwich and secured a table that afforded him privacy. He logged onto the free Wi-Fi and as soon as he had Tony's profile set up, he sent a message along with a friend request to Ginny's Facebook page. While he waited he amused himself by requesting and accepting numerous friend requests from random strangers all over the world.

He didn't have to wait long for Ginny to "friend" him and send him a suggestive hello. He returned her greeting and sent a message asking if she would like to meet regarding an income opportunity. She asked where and when. He gave her the name and address of the coffee shop, inviting her to join him. She replied that she lived in the neighborhood and would meet him in thirty minutes. He sat back, satisfied that his plan was in motion and success was within his grasp. Ginny was even more eager and trusting than he had dared to hope.

Alexander recognized the short, multi colored, spiked hair the instant she entered the coffee shop. In spite of the cool temperature, she was wearing a revealing tank top and mini skirt. Colorful skin tight leggings with knee high, black, high heeled boots completed her ensemble. The snug tank top and the cool temperature resulted in the outline of her nipples standing at attention, straining against the thin material of her top as if poised to escape. She was older and more leathery than the pictures on her Facebook page, but her appearance was not the reason Alexander had selected her. When she glanced in his direction, he nodded his head and waved to her. When she sat down, she got right to the business at hand.

"So Tony, you said you had a way for me to make some fast money. I'm interested, what have you got in mind?"

"I saw your Facebook page and thought perhaps you would be inclined to service me with... say... oral sex?"

"You a cop?"

"No."

"You have to tell me the truth if you're a cop."

"Actually, my dear lady, that's a misconception that is perpetuated by Hollywood and their overzealous screenwriters. But I assure you, I am not a police officer. Do we have a deal?"

"Depends. Out in the alley or in your car?"

"Alley."

"$25 cash, pay first."

"Agreed. I just got this coffee and croissant sandwich, you want something while I finish?"

"You buying?"

"I'm buying. Here's your $25 plus an extra $10. Go get yourself something at the counter."

"Say, you're alright Tony." Ginny appeared to relax. When she stood up, she leaned over to give Alexander a view of her bare breasts as she scooped up his money and tucked it into the small purse strapped around her waist.

"I'll take good care of you." she whispered in his ear.

When she returned to the table, Alexander took the lead and guided their conversation so he could divulge the information that he needed her to absorb. "I appreciate your agreeing to meet me today. I fear I'm at my wits end."

"So sorry to hear that Tony. I'm happy to listen, if you'd like to talk about it."

"No... I'm sure you have your own problems, you don't want to hear mine."

"Well, we have time, we're just sitting here anyway, why don't you tell me what's bothering you, if it will make you feel better, I'll charge you another $10 for listening."

Alexander pulled out another bill and set it on the table. He found it amusing, watching Ginny reach out to snatch the money and tuck it away. Reminded him of training a dog, rewarding her each time she learned a new trick. He was sure Ginny had him pegged by now for an easy mark with more money than good sense. Time to set the hook.

Alexander continued his dialogue by pretending he was distraught because his wife was seeing another man. "For about a year now she's been refusing to let me touch her. She won't have sex with me. She blamed menopause. I love her, you understand, but I'm still a healthy man with certain feelings, if you know what I mean. I tried to make my marriage work, until, well... last month I discovered she's been seeing another man. Now that's all I can think about. I feel guilty coming to you for relief, but I also think I deserve to indulge my fantasies, after all, I'm sure she is." He contorted his face into what he hoped would look like a pathetic, or better yet, a vulnerable expression. "You'll be the first woman who's touched me other than my wife in a very long time."

Ginny said very little, but was sympathetic and often reached out to pat his hand in a show of understanding.

Alexander looked away, taking his time. Letting his face show his hopeless state of mind before he switched to show indignation. "I just wish I knew someone that would beat the crap out of the little pipsqueak that's screwing my wife. I'd be willing to pay cash to watch that, if only I knew someone I could trust. I wish I could do it myself, my wife's lover is just a little fellow." Alexander paused to observe Ginny's reaction before he continued. "I suppose I could do it myself but I'm such a gentle soul. I realized long ago that I was incapable of violence. Hell, I couldn't even kill a spider in my house. Truth is, I'm sad to say, I'm one of those men who's afraid of his own shadow. I know I couldn't do it myself, but I'd be willing, grateful even, to pay someone five thousand dollars to do it, if I knew we could get away with it. Well, enough about my problems, thanks for listening. I do feel better."

Ginny seemed to show genuine concern for his problem as he pretended to pour out his heart. Alexander was sure that he saw her eyes light up when he mentioned the five thousand dollars. Well he thought, the line is set, he was sure that she had taken the bait, hook, line and sinker.

It wasn't long before they were in the alley and Ginny was demonstrating her expertise by undoing his pants and handling his "Mr. Woody" who lived up to his name as soon as it was exposed to the damp air. Alexander couldn't remember the last time anyone had touched him there. The sob story he gave her about not having sexual relations in months had been the truth.

"Where's your condom?"

"What? I don't have a condom."

"No condom sweetheart, you're going to have to pay $50 dollars more."

Alexander groaned.

"I might have one in my purse , Let me see if I can find it." she removed her hands to open her purse and started digging around.

"No, no, don't stop, I'll pay." He fumbled in his pockets until he pulled three twenty dollar bills out and waved them at her. She grabbed the bills and tucked them into her open purse.

Relief flooded his entire body as he felt her continue. He leaned back, knowing he would have emptied his pockets if she'd asked him at that point.

He forgot the purpose of his mission as he looked down to watch the top of her head bobbing. His emotions were in turmoil, his heart racing, the blood rushing through his veins. He closed his eyes and tried to control his passion. Make it last longer. He felt a tickle creeping through every part of his body, felt the pressure built to a crescendo as his body became desperate for it to stop, while his brain wanted it to last forever. He was helpless as all his tactile feelings rushed to exit his body through his penis. His internal struggles were futile, within seconds, he grabbed her head and held it tight as he leaned his body into her and exploded. It happened so quickly that they were both taken by surprise. Alexander kept his eyes closed as he surrendered to his orgasmic thrill.

"Well, I guess you really did need that Tony! Feel free to message me anytime. I live nearby." Ginny stood up, wiping her mouth on her arm as she straightened her clothing, then walked away.

He watched her as she left the alley and disappeared, unable to speak because of the thunderous beating of his heart as it continued to pump blood through his veins in double time. He was a little weak in the knees and remained leaning against the building until after she rounded the corner. He had somehow forgotten about his sexual needs. That there was more to life than death.

After another minute he adjusted himself, picked up his computer and began his long walk to where he had parked his car. He wished he would be able to visit her again when this was over but Tony Stark had to disappear into thin air once Jethro was eliminated. Now he had to wait for her to contact Jethro Mercier and then for them to contact Tony Stark.

*     *     *

At home later that day, Alexander kept Tony's Facebook page open on screen so he wouldn't miss anything. He was having fun accepting friend requests for his alter-ego. Ridiculous how many people displayed a total lack of good judgement and friended you on Facebook. He laughed. I could be a serial killer for all they knew! Wait, I am a serial killer! How delightful! These people are so ignorant and there was no particular pattern, they were a combination of different social and economic status and ages. Most wanted him to join them in an adventure game of some type.

While he waited, he pulled out his journal and brought it up to date, improving on his encounter with Ginny. He described her as a younger and more attractive version and improved his performance as well. He wanted to make sure that the people who read it would know what a virile male he was. He had her refer to him as Mr. Big, like the guy in Sex in the City.

In due course, he ran out of things to write about so he included his upcoming plans for Jethro. Documenting each swing of the bat to demonstrate the choreography that had gone into planning the event.

As the morning passed into afternoon, he waited. He heard the tone that indicated he had a new message. A quick glance and his heart began to race. It was Ginny. He read her text message; I have a friend that offered to help you with your problem. He wants to know if you are really interested in making a deal?

Alexander waited a few minutes before he answered, he didn't want to appear too anxious.

He replied: Thanks, but I'm not sure. Has he done this before? How would he do it? What would he use?

Ginny: Yes, he has. Said his fist, sometimes a bat, wants to know how you would pay him?

Alex: How about $2,000 before and $3,000 after?

Ginny: How bout half up front, half after?

Alex: Acceptable.

Ginny: Meet tonight, in person with cash and ID information on target.

Alexander was delighted, this is perfect he thought, just what I was going to suggest.

He resumed typing: Agreed, we can meet on the roof of the Travelers Hotel. Tell him to come alone.

Assure him that we will have all the privacy we will need to exchange information and first payment. Metal detectors have been installed at all the doors into the hotel so no concealed weapons. Go to the tenth floor, lock on door to roof is broken. Take stairs to the roof. Will meet on roof at 7 pm this evening.

Alexander waited. It seemed like forever before he heard the familiar beep.

Ginny: Terms accepted - 7pm tonight.

Alexander fairly jumped for joy, it had been so easy. He looked at his watch, it was only 3:30. He sighed, it was going to be a long three hours before he could leave. He already had packed a bag with fresh clothes, plastic, a container of mace, a Taser Pulse, rags, rope, duct tape, bleach and the wooden baseball bat he planned to use. He had clothing already laid out on his bed, all black with a black knit cap for his head. He hoped it would disguise him enough so he could get within the 15 feet needed for the Taser to work. He even had another pair of inexpensive footwear that he would discard after he was finished tonight. Yes, he was prepared and looking forward to killing Jethro Mercier tonight.

Time to celebrate, he thought to himself as he picked up the phone and called the Remington Restaurant. He ordered their famous Duck A L'orange, with a side of Foie Gras to go. This was going to be a most satisfying day, and he was looking forward to every second.

After finishing his superb meal, he paced around the house until his watch said 6:22. Close enough. Picking up his bag, he walked to the garage, tossed it into the back seat and got in. Backing his car out onto the street, he headed toward the hotel and started humming Stairway to Heaven. Strange, he thought, wonder what it means that there is a stairway to Heaven and a highway to Hell? Could it be an indication of which is the most traveled?

## CHAPTER 28

It was a busy afternoon of planning and preparation but everything was in place when Emma pulled into Peter's driveway at 6 o'clock. She parked and checked to make sure Mitch could hear her and she could hear him. The van was parked on East Avenue, East of Vick Park A. Officer Geraci had already scanned the inside of the house.

"There are three people inside Emma, one person in the kitchen, and two are walking toward the front door. Did you bring your Taser and your backup weapon?"

"Yes, I'm armed. I have the bug with me so he won't suspect I found it. That must be how they know I'm here. Well, here goes."

"Good luck, I'm coming in if there's any sign of trouble. Be careful Emma."

"Goes without saying, I'll signal when I want you to come in. Wait for it."

Emma got out of her car and walked to Peter's front door. Even though she knew he was waiting on the other side, she was still surprised when the door opened before she rang the door chimes.

Peter was standing next to Mrs. Kleinman, whose eyes, Emma realized were scanning the activity on the street behind her. Peter reached for Emma's hand as she stepped into his house.

"Well that was fast, I didn't even ring the bell!"

"Oh, sorry if we startled you Emma. My security alarm went off as soon as your car touched my property, so I knew you were here the second you arrived."

"Oh, of course, you must have top of the line security. I mean, with all your success, I guess you can't be too careful."

"Hope you don't find that troublesome Emma, but you're right, I do have the best security money can buy. I did mention it when we were talking about replacing the plumbing. If you remember, I told you we also did the electric and installed a security system at the same time. In fact, that is one of the things I want to talk to you about. Come in, we can sit in the parlor, I lit a fire, we'll be comfortable while we talk."

Mrs. Kleinman closed the door then stepped toward Emma. "Let me take your jacket dear. Would you like a drink before dinner?"

"Just tea, thank you. A glass of unsweetened iced tea if you have it please."

"Make that two glasses of tea."

"Very good."

Emma walked into the parlor and sat in the armchair closest to the doorway.

Peter watched her movements, then sighed. "So, I'm guessing you've uncovered my secret past. I can tell by the way you're acting Emma. Good thing you don't work undercover, you aren't a very good actress."

"What's that supposed to mean?"

"Sorry, just my unsuccessful attempt to lower the tension with humor. Truth is, my past was what I wanted to talk to you about, although I was hoping to tell you myself, before you found out by digging into my background. What have you uncovered so far?"

Emma was taken back by the casual manner Peter was offering to discuss his criminal activities and was angry at herself for having fallen for his charms. She shook it off, taking care to control the tone of her voice.

"Actually, I've discovered quite a bit, going back six years to the murder of your partner, Ryan Kelly in London." Peter remained silent. He appeared to be organizing his thoughts as he sat down on the couch opposite Emma.

Taking a deep breath, he shrugged his shoulders as if resigning himself to the inescapable truth and began speaking. "It's true Emma. Everything you heard or read about my partner, it all happen. I was going to tell you tonight. I shouldn't have put it off. I kept thinking, hoping, that if things worked out as I wanted, as I hoped they would, that it wouldn't matter to you. But I'll just tell you everything now and let the cards fall where they may."

"Wouldn't matter?" was all she could say.

Mrs. Kleinman stepped into the room carrying their beverages. Peter and Emma were silent as she placed each of their drinks on alabaster coasters from her tray and set them on the coffee table between them.

Peter broke the silence. "Mrs. Kleinman, I would like you and Gordon to join us and get yourselves something to drink as well."

"Ja, right away."

Emma's cop sense began to tingle; it would be three against one. She calculated her options. She had the advantage of knowing she had to stall only long enough to give backup time to enter the house. She hoped she would have enough evidence to put them away before that happened. She needed to stay calm if she was going to pull this off.

She heard Mitch's voice in her ear, "I don't like the sound of this Em, we got your back. Just get him to confess and we're coming in."

Peter's eyes locked with hers and she realized she didn't see a killer looking back at her, she saw sadness mixed with fatigue and longing. Peter cleared his throat. "I met Ryan Kelly in college, he was my friend for 13 years before his death. We started our business together after college. He was your typical charming Irishman… and he was a criminal. He got involved with smuggling and arms dealing, using our company as cover. It was small at first, then he found himself involved with some really bad people who forced him into major crimes. When they wanted to escalate into drugs and human trafficking, he wanted out." Peter glanced at the doorway. "Ah, here comes Gordon. He will be able to shed more light on the events at this point. Gordon, please come in and tell Emma what happened to Ryan."

"Are you certain, Mr. Hartman? She's an officer of the law."

"Yes, I know. Tell her what happened, please."

Gordon was still hesitant. Mrs. Kleinman reached for his hand and the two of them sat down on the couch. He looked again at Peter who nodded. "Go ahead, Gordon."

"Yes Sir, well, it started about 9 years ago. Mr. Kelly hired me to be his bodyguard back in Ireland. Over the years we became gut... excuse me, good friends. I didn't know about the criminal activities he was involved in 'til he came to me for help getting out. He told me everything. How it had started small, just doing a bloke a favor smuggling a trinket for his daughter. Mr. Kelly said he was well compensated, then another und another 'till he found himself in the middle of a sophisticated smuggling operation. He told me everything, gave me documents he had compiled listing names of everyone he worked with, where the guns were und how they moved them. He explained the terrible situation he was faced with und asked me if I could help him get out from under. I've contacts in London, und sent him there, where I thought he would be out of danger temporarily, 'till I could work out a plan. While he was in London, they found him und had him killed." Kleinman looked into his wife's eyes before he continued. "I sent Vera home on the first flight to Germany to keep her safe."

"Ja, that's the truth," she confirmed.

"Then I went to London to see what I could discover. I uncovered a plan to kill Mr. Hartman in an attempt to take over his company. I sent an anonymous tip to the police in Ireland that included all the information I had up to that point. I told them where the last shipment was stored und all the names Mr. Kelly said were involved, including our own warehouse personnel. Then I flew into New York City praying that I would arrive in time to save Mr. Hartman's life."

"That's right Emma. That's where I come into the picture. I was in New York City on business when I got the news about Ryan's death. I was in my hotel room, making preparations to leave when I answered a knock at my door and Gordon was standing there. He stepped in and told me everything that he just told you. He said he would stay with me and do his best to protect my life. Minutes later, the door flew open and a man with a gun walked in. Gordon knew him as Accidental Al. I think Al was surprised to see I wasn't alone, but he was committed at that point. He motioned with his gun for us to move into the bathroom. Gordon took advantage of that movement to jump him. The gun went off and I was hit in the ribs, just missing my heart and lungs. Al dropped his gun and ran. I lay on the floor, doubled over in excruciating pain, unable to move. Gordon grabbed a small pillow and put it on my wound, wrapped my arms around it and told me to hold tight. He called 911, notified hotel security, then grabbed the gun and left to find the man who had killed Ryan."

"Ja, that's right," Gordon concurred. Emma saw Vera squeeze his hand again. "I lost him that night, but I had a couple contacts in the city und through them I discovered where Al was staying. The next night, I was sitting outside the house when I saw two men go to the door. They came out a few minutes later with Al. I followed them to the pier und was waiting for my opportunity to confront him. Instead, I watched as they tied him to a piling, gagged him, stabbed him several times in the legs und disappeared into the shadows to watch him die. I remained hidden und I watched Al struggle until the tide finally rose enough to drown him. I waited another fifteen or twenty minutes until I knew they had left, then threw Al's gun into the water not far from where I knew he was und left."

Emma shuddered again, visualizing that not one, but three people had witnessed that horrible death.

"But why would these two men have wanted Al dead?"

"Tying up loose ends, I figured. When the Harbor Police raided the warehouse und arrested some of the people connected with the smuggling ring, the ringleader had to act fast before he or his organization were connected to Mr. Kelly's murder. No telling who Al could have implicated. They had to eliminate him, und they just happened to hire sadistic men that enjoyed their work."

"Do you know who the men were that killed Al?"

"Nein, und I couldn't find out. That's why I stayed here and why Peter hired Vera und I to continue to protect him. We knew that most of the people involved were arrested, but we still didn't know who was running the operation. As the years went by with no further attempts on Mr. Hartman's life, we assumed that Peter Hartman Enterprises was no longer a desirable commodity. To a great extent because the British, Irish and American FBI have kept us under close surveillance.

"Were there any further attempts on your life, Peter?"

"No. Plus I took additional steps that I hoped would eliminate any reason for them to want me dead. With Gordon's help, I terminated everyone that we thought might have been involved. I moved all my business interest out of Ireland. I hired a new firm to head our overseas security. I have standing orders for management to cooperate with foreign authorities and the F.B.I. whenever they suspect our company of anything illegal. In hindsight, I think their unannounced inquiries and searches over the last five years have provided additional safety for me and for my company."

"Then why do you have Gordon and Vera still employed as your bodyguards, even though you claim you have nothing to worry about?"

"Well, he did save my life Emma. Plus, he and Vera had always dreamed of living in the United States so I offered them both positions as my bodyguard. A couple years later Gordon told me of his secret dream of becoming a chef. I transitioned his position to include working as my executive chef. Now he supervises the kitchens and all special events for myself and my company. Vera, it turned out, is a talented baker so I put her in charge of bakery operations."

"So why do they still live here with you?"

"At first it was because I wanted them close by, for my protection. Now it's because they want to live here. It's an arrangement that works for us. Emma, I'm not a criminal, I'm proud to say I'm an honest man. I had no prior knowledge of my partner's dealings. Ryan Kelly was a good man who made bad choices that he ultimately paid for with his life."

The four of them sat in silence. The only sound was an antique clock ticking on the mantle. Then Emma remembered the bug. She reached into her purse and pulled out the baggie with the bug inside.

"Then how do you explain this bug you gave me?"

Peter reached for the baggie. "What is this? What kind of bug is it?" Peter looked it over and passed it to Gordon. "Do you know anything about this, Gordon?"

"Nein, I've never seen it before."

"Emma. where did you find this?" Peter asked.

"In the Trojan Horse you gifted me! The St. Michael medal! I don't see how you can sit there and tell me you know nothing about it when it was concealed inside the gift you so gallantly hung around my neck! With instructions to wear it always! 'No strings attached', was what you said!"

"Emma, I purchased that necklace and medallion myself from, **JF Jones Jewelers,** at Stoneridge Plaza. My family has done business with their family for three generations. I trust them completely.

Peter's eyes drifted as he contemplated the different possibilities. "I planned to have it engraved and said so to my neighbor when I bought it. Alexander said he had a personal engraver who did exquisite work and would rush it so I would have it in time for our date, so I let him take care of it." Peter paused again in thought, "I gave it to him. It doesn't make sense, but Alexander is the only person that could have tampered with it. He has been a little off since his parents were murdered, but I can't imagine why he would want to track you? I don't understand."

"Peter, tell me more about how his parents died."

"I don't know much more than what I already told you. They were beaten to death with a bat. Apparently his parents returned home and interrupted a man robbing their house. His father must have caught the man in the upstairs bedroom and confronted him. They think Alexander's mother heard the commotion and ran up to see what was happening. She must have seen her husband on the floor bleeding, and ran into another room to call 911. They think the intruder followed her, and smashed her head in before she could complete the call. They both died of blunt force trauma and bled to death in the upstairs bedrooms. Police caught the guy by tracing a piece of the pawned jewelry back to him. Police got a confession, but when his attorneys had the confession tossed during the trial, the case fell apart. He was released. Alexander's never been the same. He had a breakdown and was in a private hospital for months. No telling how that kind of trauma affects a person. At times, he seems to live in an alternative world, but I am positive, he's harmless. He believes in our criminal justice system, in fact, he was working on his Master's Degree in Criminal Justice and Forensic Science when this happened."

"So he's knowledgeable about police procedures. That's interesting. Do you know what type of car he drives?"

"A Lincoln, why?"

"I would very much like to talk to him about this bug. Do you think we could go to his house to talk to him right now?"

"Sure, he should be home, he usually is. Gordon, hold supper."

"Certainly, sir."

Emma heard Mitch in her earbud. "Emma, it all fits, the lab just identified the location receiving the transmissions from the bug. It's inside Alexander Wright's house. I called for more backup and a warrant. I'll have officer Geraci wait for the warrant and I'll meet you at Wright's front door unless you have a different plan."

"Okay, good plan. Peter do you have a key to Alexander's house in case he won't open the door?"

"Yeah, he gave it to me before he was sent away. Asked me to keep an eye on the house for him."

"Great, so you have permission to enter. Grab the key and come with me. Mitch, we'll be right there."

"Did you just call me Mitch?"

Emma ignored Peter's question. "Get the key! Get the key!" She heard Mitch in her earbud. "Hold on Emma, we can't bring a civilian into this situation, It could be dangerous."

"We have no choice! Without a warrant, we may need Peter to let us in."

The mantle clock chimed. It was exactly 6:30 when Emma and Peter ran out of his house. They rounded the corner and dashed up the porch stairs to the front door of Alexander's house. Mitch appeared right behind them.

Peter looked at Mitch, then Emma. "Now I get it. Can't say I blame you for being wary. You are a cop, after all."

"Self-preservation, given your history, I'm sure you can appreciate some healthy skepticism on my part. Knock on my signal Peter." Mitch and Emma stood to either side of the door with their guns drawn as Emma motioned for Peter to knock. She listened but heard no resulting sounds from inside the house. She nodded her head a second time, signaling Peter to knock again. She counted on her fingers to five, then had Peter call out for Alexander to open the door. Still no sound from inside the house. A patrol car pulled up with lights flashing, and two patrolmen ran up to the door with their guns drawn. Emma motioned for one of them to cover the back and the other to stay in front. Emma signaled Peter to unlock the door.

When it swung open, Mitch moved in first, followed by Emma. She stopped when she realized Peter had followed them in. "Go back out to the porch and wait while we clear the house."

He shook his head. "No, Alex is my friend, I'll be able to help if he's in here. I know he's harmless."

"Damn it, listen to me! Go back outside. Now!"

"I let you in. I'm staying with you."

Emma didn't have time to argue. "Fine, stay close." She heard Mitch yell, "clear", from somewhere in the back of the house.

Another car rolled up and two more officers joined them. The officers came to the front door and looked to Emma for direction.

"Help my partner finish clearing the house officers. Peter, follow me, we're going to check out Alexander's office.

Emma carefully opened the doors to the study and cleared the room. "CLEAR! Geraci, can you still hear me?"

"Yes ma'am. I'm waiting for the warrant. It's signed and being faxed as we speak."

"Good work, put in a call for Jack's crew and tech support. I've got a computer and a laptop in here."

Mitch walked into the study, "No sign of Wright. Car's not in the garage, leftover dishes in the dining room. Looks like he enjoyed a duck dinner before he left the house. Patrol's searching the upstairs. What did you find in here?"

"Looks like he was writing in this journal." Emma picked up the open journal from the desk and started glancing through it. She skimmed quickly through the handwritten pages. "Wow, I don't believe this. He's documented everything that he's done so far in minute detail. How he shot Maxwell! My God, I don't believe it - here is how he staged Jackson's suicide! Here's a new one, name of Mercier."

"Oh my God!" Peter exclaimed, "are you referring to the recent murders you were investigating? You think Alexander was involved in those killings? Emma! Jethro Mercier is the guy that killed his parents, what does it say about him?"

"Mercier's in the last few pages here. Oh no, what time is it?" she asked? Mitch and Peter both looked at their watches and answered, "six forty-four".

"Peter take your key and go home. Mitch with me! He's meeting Mercier at 7 tonight!" Emma ran out of the house carrying the journal in her hand. She jumped into the passenger side of the nearest patrol car, Mitch slid into the driver's side. He turned on the lights and sirens as he headed the car toward downtown.

Emma put her finger on her earbud, "Geraci! Can you still hear me?"

"Yes ma'am"

"Take charge until Jack's unit gets there, make sure you keep everything sealed up tight until then."

"Yes ma'am,"

"He'll do a good job; it should be routine." Emma pictured him jumping out of the van to take over the entire operation with the energy and enthusiasm only the young possess. She pulled the earbud out and disconnected the wire she was wearing while Mitch called for backup.

"Tell them to meet us at the Travelers Hotel on Main Street." Emma continued reading the last pages of the journal, hoping to spot any information that might help them prevent another murder.

"According to this, we need to get to the roof of the hotel, that's where he plans on killing Mercier, with a bat."

"Got it. Hang on, Emma, busy intersection ahead."

Emma continued studying the journal as Mitch weaved in and out of traffic, closing the distance between them and a serial killer.

## CHAPTER 29

Alexander parked his car two blocks from the hotel. He knew there were cameras in the hotel garage because this was one of the many properties that his father had once owned. It seemed like so many years ago that he been an innocent child playing cops and robbers in the lobby… always playing the cop who was fighting imaginary robbers. He sighed, it was so long ago, seemed like a lifetime.

He walked past the illuminated entrance to the hotel, around to the alley that ran alongside. He slipped in a side door located off the alley, walked down the stairs into the basement and rode the service elevator to the 10th floor. He felt his adrenaline surging as the elevator rose. He could barely contain his excitement as he moved closer to his quarry. When the elevator stopped and the doors opened, he was quivering with anticipation. He had to settle his nerves before he continued. The roof was right above him. He walked past the door leading to the roof and moved to the end of the hallway, to the floor length windows. He stood there taking deep breaths in and out as he struggled to control his sudden case of nerves.

A flash of light from the street below caught his attention. He was startled as he realized the flashing lights were police cars pulling up in front of the hotel entrance. One, two, three of them. He wondered what was happening. Why they were there. What unforeseen event had triggered this devastating coincidence? The hair on the back of his neck tingled when he saw Emma Mason jump out of a police car and run toward the front door, followed by her partner and more police.

He froze, his mind went blank and then the thoughts raced through his brain in triple time. How did she find me! How could this happen? She can't stop me now! I'm too close! This can't be happening!

He looked at the elevator and realized she was already on her way up to the 10th floor. His mind flew through the possibilities, but none would work. He was trapped like an animal. Heart racing, he headed for the stairs. He couldn't just stand there waiting for her to corner him, he had to move. He opened the door and started up the two flights that would take him to the roof and his prey.

That's right, he reminded himself, you're the hunter, you have the advantage here. He burst through the door and out onto the roof where he spotted his target standing there, waiting for him. Waiting to die.

## CHAPTER 30

Jethro Mercer had arrived much earlier to give himself time to check out the location when he was going to meet Tony Stark. He wanted time to explore their meeting place and secure the area so he would be in control of the encounter. Ginny had already described Tony to him. Too much of a coward to confront the man that was screwing his wife. What a lightweight this man was, he wouldn't last an hour in the world Jethro grew up in. Jethro hoped that Tony would be stupid enough to bring all the money and he would just rob him, but then, he really did enjoy beating people. Perhaps he would do both.

Well, he could decide after he met Tony whether he would help him or just rob him outright. Jethro had found a secure spot across from the door, where he could hide in the shadows while he waited. He could observe Tony when he walked through the door onto the roof.

He was standing in the shadows, when he heard first one siren wailing, then another, the unmistakable sound of police cars rushing through the streets. Curiosity got the best of him as the blare of the sirens called to him like the winged creatures whose singing lured unwary sailors to their deaths.

They sounded like they were coming closer. He abandoned his secure position and walked over to the edge of the roof so he could look down and watch as the police cars pulled up to the front of the hotel. He wondered what was going on, but he wasn't concerned. He had done nothing in the last couple of weeks that would have interested the police. Not this much anyway, he shook his head and smiled. He watched as another police car pulled up. He was wondering how many of them would show up and why, when he heard the door to the roof open. He looked up, but he only saw a man dressed all in black, carrying a bag, backlit by the light from the staircase.

He waited, thinking only of all the money in that bag, all that easy money that would soon be his. Maybe he would treat Ginny to a nice dinner when this was over. This was all thanks to her, she was always finding opportunities for making money without working hard. Yes, he must remember to thank her for this.

# CHAPTER 31

Alexander heard the fire door open on the 10th floor and knew Emma was just seconds behind him. He forced himself to focus on his prey. There he was, Jethro, standing right in front of him… the miserable piece of garbage who killed his parents, standing on the edge of the roof.

He wished for the luxury of more time. Time to explain to the detective the reasoning behind his decision. If she knew, she'd understand. But he didn't have time to think. He felt angry frustration mixing violently with adrenaline induced fury. He was so close he couldn't get his brain to function.

He saw Mercier turn and look at him. He forced himself to act casually as he moved closer to his prey.

"Hey Jethro, how about all those cops, right?"

"Yeah! What the fuck man? You know what's going on?"

"Who knows. Prostitution sting is my guess."

As Alexander drew close, their eyes met and Alexander saw a flash of recognition. Instantly a new plan flew into his mind born on wings of pure hate and desperation. Alexander dropped the bag he was carrying and charged straight at Mercier, running as fast as he could. They were facing each other when their bodies collided. Alexander's momentum turning his body into a wrecking ball, smashing into Jethro with enough force to uproot him and send both of them flying off the roof and into the night air.

The door to the roof flew open, casting a spotlight on them as their bodies merged into one dark shape of tangled arms and legs before they dropped out of sight.

Jethro's scream was so loud it pierced Alexander's ears. He continued to hold tight as Jethro flailed his arms in a pitiful effort to stop the free fall.

Alexander smiled and held fast as they both continued falling. He was awash with the pleasure of personally removing Jethro Mercier from this world. He was flush with satisfaction. He knew Mother would be proud. Who could say he was crazy now?

He would die a hero.

## CHAPTER 32

Emma ran out with her gun drawn. "Police, stop where you are!" she shouted just as the tangled bodies flew off the solid roof into the empty night air, then disappeared from view.

She watched uncomprehending. Thinking she had imagined it, but as she started running toward the edge she heard screaming and realized what she had seen was real. Unbelievable, but real. When she reached the edge of the roof, she looked down just in time to see the black shadow that had been two living breathing human beings land and spread out into an artistic pattern of splatter.

She saw the officers pushing people back, off the sidewalk. Some people were looking up, others looking down, hiding their faces.

"My God Mitch, I didn't see that coming."

"No way anyone could have. Wright was crazy as they come, the man was certifiable."

"You're right, he was so bent on revenge that he was willing to do anything. Even kill himself."

Emma turned and directed her attention to the officers that had reached the roof. She shouted orders and collected evidence. She took comfort in the routine procedures of securing and recording the evidence.

Even though they had been too late to stop him from killing one last time, she was thankful no innocent people had been crushed when the bodies landed on the concrete sidewalk, in front of the busy hotel entrance.

When Emma and Mitch had finished on the roof they returned to the sidewalk. The coroner's team had been called and were in the process of cleaning up, using trowels to scrape body parts off the sidewalk. The pieces large enough to move to the morgue had been tagged and removed. The team continued securing and identifying every minute piece of the two bodies that had splattered in all directions when they hit.

Doc MacGee was there supervising. He walked over to Emma and Mitch when he saw them standing on the sidewalk. "Mitch, why don't you and Emma go home, there's nothing left for you to do here. Bottom line is, these two guys failed miserably at their attempt to imitate Superman. Wonder if they knew Superman is a work of fiction? Hey, maybe they thought they would get a do over?"

"Really Doc, making jokes?"

"Yea. How could I resist? Seriously, you guys go home and get some rest, you've had a long day."

Mitch shrugged his shoulders, looked at Emma and said, "I could use some food, how about you Emma?"

## CHAPTER 33

It had been a week since Emma had witnessed the two men hurtling off the roof to their death. She could still hear the bloodcurdling scream from the unwilling participant as he plunged to his demise with Alexander holding him in a death grip. Her mind replayed the memory of looking down just as the two bodies hit the pavement. It was a sight that inspired nightmares in otherwise untroubled minds.

Emma was still dealing with the required paperwork so she could close this case and put it away for good. She hoped the physical act of putting these evidence boxes and files into storage would help ease the memories. Trouble was, this case was connected to so many other open cases and they each needed to be documented and closed out, one by one. Mitch walked into her office eating a chocolate glazed donut and carrying a cup of coffee.

Emma took in a deep breath so she could enjoy the fragrant aroma of coffee and pastry that seemed to envelop Mitch every morning like his own, personal cologne.

"Mind if I eat a snack while we go over these files?" He moved the chair closer to her desk before sitting down.

"If I said no?"

"Well then I'd have to shove it all in at once!"

"You would too, wouldn't you!"

"You know me so well. So, what's still left to go over?"

"I'm not putting this into any of the reports mind you, but I've been wondering if we would have caught Alexander if he hadn't kept a written record of every detail of his murders?"

"You're asking me if I think he executed the elusive, perfect murders they talk about on TV?"

"Yeah. Do you think we would have caught him if he hadn't planted that bug on me?"

"Well, Em… I won't deny that helped, but we were on to him. He tried to disguise his killings as suicides and we saw through that after his second kill. The perfect murder, in my opinion, would mean that we were oblivious that a murder had taken place, therefore, we would not even be looking for a murderer."

"According to his journal he was sure he had succeeded in disguising the deaths as suicides. Do you believe this title? *Adventures in Murder*. Makes it sound like a Sherlock Holmes story. Didn't even try to make the text mysterious or obscure. Just so predictable, don't you think?"

"Yeah, except I don't remember any Sherlock Holmes stories where the murderer ends his own life so he could eliminate his victim. Not a good career choice for a budding serial killer."

"You're forgetting about Holmes and Moriarty going over the Reichenbach Falls in *The Final Problem*. We know from his book that Alexander hadn't planned to end his life that way. He changed his plan when he realized we were right behind him. Bet that was a surprise. According to his journal here, he didn't think much of my expertise as a detective."

"Smart as he was Emma, he seriously underestimated you and our ability to find him and stop him."

"He didn't believe we would want to stop him. He was sure we would be grateful that he was able to eliminate killers that the courts had not been able to bring to justice."

"Like I said, he was smart but he was still off his rocker. About as crazy as they get."

"The only thing I'll be grateful for is when all this paperwork is completed and I can get out from behind this desk."

"I don't know why you're complaining. At least you have a window in your office. Mine is in the middle of the building with no window. I would be willing to give up donuts for a week if I could work in an office with a window."

"You, give up donuts? What would you eat if you couldn't eat donuts?" They both looked up when they heard a loud knock at Emma's door. Mitch jumped up from his chair to open it.

"Hey Donnie, what are you doing in our neck of the woods?"

"Mitch." The man said as he extended his hand.

"Emma, I'd like you to meet special agent Don Newcomb, he's my contact at the FBI."

Emma stood up and offered her hand. "Pleased to meet you, special agent Newcomb, and thanks for backing up my operation on the Hartman case. Sorry it didn't work out the way you had hoped."

"That's why I'm here. To thank you both for your help, especially you Emma, for wearing the wire. We closed out our case on Peter Hartman, his company, and his employees, Gordon and Vera Kleinman. Everything they told you checked out. Looks like we were wrong about his company continuing to be involved in any type of ongoing criminal activities. I dropped off my final report to your Captain, plus I sent copies to Homeland and Scotland Yard. It clears Peter Hartman Enterprises on all counts."

"Well, it was my pleasure working with the FBI. Anytime we can help."

"Don, are you going to be in town for long?" Mitch asked, "Maybe we could get together for dinner and drinks? A little celebration perhaps?"

"Sorry Mitch, I'd love to but I'm flying out in three hours, crisis elsewhere. Have to keep moving. Putting out fires before they're out of control. Maybe next time I'm in Rochester."

"Looking forward to it, stay safe Don."

"Stay in touch, Mitch."

They shook hands again as he left the office. Mitch looked at Emma to see how she was handling this new information. "Well, what do you think Emma? Are you still interested in seeing Peter now that he's been cleared of any wrongdoing?"

"I don't know, Mitch. I've had so many confusing thoughts about him since last week. First he was just this very charming gentleman that was making all the right moves, swept me off my feet. Then I learn about his past. I get wired and go into his house bent on exposing him. I don't think I can ever look him in the eye again. Besides, why would he want to see me again? I believed the worst of him. I was ready to send him to jail for the rest of his life. I'm not surprised that I haven't heard from him since that night."

"I'm sure you will Emma and you'll know what to do when the time comes. Meanwhile, what's left? Isn't it time to box this up and file it away?"

"We just need to add Doc's report and Jack's CU report to our files and we'll be done."

"Sounds good. I'll call them and check to see what time will work for them. Love to put it away today." Mitch finished scribbling in his notebook and walked out. He called a few minutes later and reported that they could see Doc now and Jack would be available after lunch. Emma met Mitch in front of the staircase and they walked down to the basement together. Emma knocked on Doc's office door, then they walked in. Emma moved to her favorite overstuffed chair and sat down. She watched Mitch drop down onto the comfortable couch, stretching out his body as he put his feet up on the coffee table.

Doc opened a large file on his desk. "Make yourselves comfortable. I've concluded my examination on the remains of the bodies we recovered from the sidewalk. Using dental records, fingerprints and DNA evidence, I have determined that they were the bodies of Alexander Wright the Third, and Jethro Mercier. From the way the bodies were intertwined, I have concluded that Alexander Wright was holding onto Jethro Mercier as they fell. I used the impulse-momentum theorem to calculate the force required to propel the bodies to their final positions on the sidewalk."

"Could you translate to English please?" interrupted Mitch.

"Certainly." Doc chuckled, "You are probably more familiar with Newton's second law of motion, which is also an accepted method of measurement. Regardless of the method, my findings agree with your statements concerning what you witnessed. It is my final determination that Alexander rushed Jethro from about 15 to 20 feet away, at a force approximate to the weight of the bodies. Causing their bodies to be projected into the air and ultimately landing where they did. My conclusion is that Alexander Wright killed Jethro Mercier and himself by deliberately forcing both of them off the roof, causing them to fall 10 stories, to their deaths."

Emma nodded her approval. "That's great Doc. Now we've established their identity and how they died. Alexander's journal gives us the why. He believed he was avenging his parents' deaths at the hand of Jethro Mercier after the courts failed to convict."

"My expertise is medical, not profiling, but I bet if you had a psychological profile done, it would find Alexander Wright fit the classic pattern of a highly functioning, highly intelligent sociopath who was motivated, or triggered, when his parents were murdered."

"It sounds like a fancy way to say he was just plain crazy." Mitch said.

"Have you found next of kin for either of the men?" Emma inquired.

"Jethro Mercier had a Grandmother I found, but when I contacted her she just said good riddance to a useless human being. She said he had no other friends or relatives besides her and she wanted nothing to do with the remains."

"What about Alexander Wright?"

"No relatives there either. His wallet had an emergency contact name of Peter Hartman. I contacted him and he made arrangements to have the remains picked up three days ago."

Emma was surprised, but said nothing. She exchanged glances with Mitch who raised his eyebrows and shrugged his shoulders.

Doc MacGee asked, "is there something I should know, Emma?"

"It's not important, Doc," Mitch answered for Emma. "So the county is stuck with the abandoned body of Mercier?"

"I'm afraid so. It happens more often than you'd think. Once a family has abandoned the person while they are alive, they seldom feel any obligation when they are informed of the actual death. I'll inform the Public Administrator's office and they'll make the necessary arrangements."

There was a quick tap, tap, tap at the office door just before it opened and Doc's wife Carole swept into the room carrying a large picnic basket. "Hello everyone." she sang out as she waved her hand at Emma and Mitch. She moved to Doc's side and planted a big kiss on the top of his head.

Doc swung around in his chair so he could stand up and give her a proper kiss on the lips. "You're right on time, sweetheart. Let me take that basket, we'll just put it over here for now. Emma, Mitch, you remember my wife Carole. I forgot to eat breakfast or bring my lunch today, so she decided to pack a brunch and bring it down here for us to share." Doc stood back and gazed at his wife with undisguised admiration while she turned her attention to Emma.

"Have you heard the news?" she asked. "Our Jenny is going to have a baby, in just three and a half months. We are so excited, it's our first grandchild you know. So much to do. I'll be caring for the baby when Jenny goes back to work. I'm redecorating one room in our house as a nursery so the baby will feel right at home when we babysit. It's so exciting. A whole new chapter in our lives."

"Congratulations," Mitch and Emma said in unison. Emma continued, "We have everything we need Doc, thank you. Good seeing you again Carole and best wishes with your grandchild."

"Congrats again." Mitch repeated as they left Doc's office and headed to the stairs. "That will be one lucky baby judging by how excited they are. I never knew my grandparents but I know enough to know I missed out. How about you Emma?"

"I still have both my grandmothers and you're right, they are very special people. I'll meet you in Jack's office at two."

"Emma, could you finish up without me? There's a case in court today that I'd like to follow up on. I might need to testify and I want to talk to the D.A. beforehand."

"Sure. I'll call if I need you, otherwise we'll talk tomorrow."

Jack was in his office with his reports ready when Emma walked in at 2 o'clock.

"Why are there three files, Jack?"

"The smaller one is your serial killer, Alexander Wright the third. There wasn't much for us to investigate after he flew off the hotel roof. His journal explained everything, he left no question unanswered. I can appreciate a man who's that methodical. I dare say, he would've made a good forensic scientist if he hadn't decided to take the path to the dark side."

"The path to the dark side? You been watching Star Wars again?"

"Yep! My boys love those movies; I can quote them in my sleep."

"Great! So, what's in the big file?"

"That details all the crimes that robbery and my unit cleared up after Alexander murdered Luther Maxwell. Have to admit, we cleared up a lot of open cases and returned hundreds of dollars in stolen property to the rightful owners. Was nice to work with grateful taxpayers for a change. Kind of makes all those sleepless nights worthwhile, know what I mean?"

"Yes, I understand. Those rare days the public thanks us for what we do, makes all the hard work seem worthwhile. I do love my job, but it is always nice when the public shows us we're appreciated."

"The smallest file is Jethro Mercier's. He was suspected of several other murders besides the Wright family. All in all, Alexander eliminated some pretty bad dudes. So that's it Emma, you can close the files on these three cases."

"Thanks Jack, great job as always. Tell Anne I said hello."

Back in her office, Emma filled out the inventory sheets as she took one last look at each of the files before putting them into their individual boxes. When she finished, she sealed and labeled each of the boxes and loaded them onto the cart and took them down to the file room for permanent storage. When she returned to her office, it was after five. Time to head home, she thought. She smiled as she looked at her clean desk, then stretched out her upper body as if a heavy weight had been removed from her shoulders. She was glad to put these cases to rest. She was looking forward to going home tonight, and thought about relaxing after her workout with a nice hot bubble bath.

She wondered if she would ever cross paths with Peter again, or if a soothing bubble bath was the only hot experience she could look forward to in her immediate future! She arched and stretched her body one more time, then on a whim, she bent over to touch her toes. She spotted a white piece of paper under her desk. Getting on her hands and knees, she reached out to retrieve it.

It felt thicker than a piece of paper. She pulled it out to where she could examine it. It was dirty and there was a footprint on the flap of the envelope. She turned it over and saw her name printed on it. There was no indication to tell her how long it had been under her desk, or where it had come from. She opened it and slipped out a card. There was a sad faced puppy dog on the front.

She opened it and read:

## Can we talk? Peter.

Next in the series:

DOMESTIC JUSTICE

Eileen La Martina was humming a happy tune while she finished washing her dinner dishes. She was thinking about her boyfriend who had promised that he would visit tonight. She hoped he would be able to stay for a while this time. Eileen loved it when he stayed with her all night, but since he was married, that didn't happen very often. She knew she just had to be patient. He would tell his wife and kids eventually and then they could be together all the time.

She glanced at her smart phone sitting on the counter. She wasn't expecting anyone to call so when she finished her dishes, she shut it off and plugged it in to recharge. She continued humming while she spruced up her small apartment, sprayed some perfume on her bed pillows then ran her hand over the covers to hand iron the wrinkles.

She had already showered and applied her makeup because she wanted to be ready when he knocked on her door. She had dressed in her new skinny jeans that she bought because he said he thought they would look good on her. She put on her favorite shirt and admired the way it draped over her ample breasts. She knew it could be minutes or it might be hours, but however long, the wait would be worth it once he held her in his strong arms again. She couldn't explain it, but he made her feel so safe and protected when he held her close.

She closed her eyes and twirled around holding her arms out as if he was there with her and they were dancing at their wedding. She opened her eyes and looked up into his blue eyes looking back at her from the picture on her bookshelf. He certainly was handsome in his police uniform.

"Damn, you are so good looking!" She said out loud, "I'm such a lucky girl." She picked up the picture and continued to twirl around her bedroom singing. "Oh you must have been a beautiful baby, cause baby, look at you now."

When she heard the three familiar taps on her door, her heart skipped a beat. She set the picture down on the nearest shelf as she glanced quickly into her mirror to check her hair. She smoothed down a few strands that were out of place and threw her reflection an affectionate kiss. As she slowly moved to the door, she heard the next two taps. Her elation peaked as she waited at the door for the final tap of their prearranged signal.

When she heard it, she smiled happily as she unlocked the door and threw it open.

It took her a second to realize her mistake. She tried to close the door but it was too late, the stranger had already barreled into the apartment and pushed her away from the door before closing and locking it.

"Who are you?" She asked as calmly as she could while she backed away. She remembered the lessons she learned from her father, to always stay calm and talk to the attacker. Make him see you as a person, not an object.

"Relax," he said in a soothing voice that was at the same time, cold and unemotional. "I just want to talk with your boyfriend. Is he here yet?"

"No," she replied slowly, finding some comfort in the realization that he was not there for her.

"What do you want with him?"

"We've got business to discuss. By the way, do you know he's a married man with kids?"

"So, how's that any of your business?" she replied, as anger began to replace the panic coursing through her body. She took a good look at the stranger now. He was dressed as a phone repairman and he carried a black tool bag that clanked loudly when he dropped it on her floor. Her leg brushed the couch as she continued backing away. Her gaze fell on the old landline phone that had come with the apartment. It was setting on the table at the end of the couch. The phone, she thought, I'll call the police.

"I'll call him for you and see when he will be here," she offered, hoping she didn't sound too eager. "What did you say your name was?" She took two more steps away from the stranger and reached for the phone.

He moved toward her and smiled at her as she lifted the receiver and heard nothing. No dial tone, the line was dead.

Frightened now, she decided her best option was if she screamed for help, someone might hear her. She sucked in air to scream but his hands were around her neck, cutting off her voice before she could make a sound. She couldn't breathe. She felt his hands tighten as her body fell onto the couch. He moved with her as she fell, leaning against the couch for balance. With the phone still in her hand, she swung it wildly at his head but felt it fly out of her hand as the cord became stretched to its limit and recoiled. She clutched desperately at his gloved hands that held tightly to her throat but she couldn't budge them.

Her eyes were open, staring at the ceiling. She didn't feel any pain, which she thought was strange. Nothing hurt. She looked again at the ceiling and thought to herself, this is the last thing I will see before I die… then she closed her eyes.

He held tight for another minute, then with a quick jerk, he snapped her neck. Then he began to remove the clothing from her limp body.

# BIO

Acclaimed Author, J. A. Goodman was born and raised in Rochester, New York. She grew up on the shores of Lake Ontario and graduated from Charlotte High School. Divorced after 13 years of marriage, she raised four unique and independent children while building a career at Eastman Kodak Company as a Quality Control Technician. There she refined her writing skills by authoring technical reports, publications and training manuals. She attended evening classes at Rochester Institute of Technology and Monroe Community College. At 47, she began attending community college full time and in 1991 received an Associate of Applied Science Degree in Marketing, *with distinction.* She is currently retired and enrolled at Osher Lifelong Learning Institute of RIT, continuing to take writing courses. *Tangled Justice,* an *Emma Mason Mystery* was first released in 2016. It's success inspired *Domestic Justice* in 2017 and *Legal Justice* in 2018.

# ABOUT THE AUTHOR

As far back as I have memories, I wanted to write. I loved to read and would lose myself in the characters and stories that became real, as my imagination worked in conjunction with the author to make the characters come alive. Over the years I made many attempts at writing a novel. My first attempt was at the age of 9 when I began a book I titled *The Bobbsey Twins in Canada*. Plagiarism was not a word I was familiar with. I continued to create storylines and characters, but life kept getting in the way, and they ultimately fell by the wayside. Writing this novel to entertain others was a lifelong ambition. Always on the to do list, always at the bottom. In 2004 I attended MCC with my granddaughter Amanda and we both took a creative writing class taught by Professor Chris Perri. I wrote a short story with a surprise ending titled, *Turning Point*. Professor Perri said that it would make a great beginning to a book and he wanted an autographed copy when it was published. In 2014, I joined Osher Lifelong Learning at RIT. Attending the Memoirs and Creative writing classes. I retrieved that short story from Mr. Perri's class and began this book. I spent the next year and a half creating and writing my manuscript, using my computer and that wonderful invention, spell check. I created 46 characters and since it was a murder mystery, I also ended some of their lives as easily as I had created them. I found I had a flare for not only storytelling, but murder as well, thankfully only as an author. Twelve years had passed, but I was proud to hand him my first novel, *Tangled Justice*. I hope you enjoy it.

Email:

jagoodman2016@gmail.com

CPSIA information can be obtained
at www.ICGtesting.com
Printed in the USA
LVHW04s1827010818
585616LV00014B/1087/P

9 781537 558844